THAT YEAR AT THE OFFICE

Five members of the staff sit in the office
of a weekly magazine. There is Kate, the
photographer, Sam, who provides the
"Questions and Answers" feature,
Vicky who edits the film page, Rawden,
the Australian reporter and "Auntie"
who handles the personal advice column.
Suddenly, these five, *that* year at the
office, all fall in love with unsuitable
people. They seem to "catch" love, as if
it were an infectious illness, leaving
devastation in its wake.

THAT YEAR AT THE OFFICE

That Year At The Office

by
Rosemary Timperley

MAGNA PRINT BOOKS
Long Preston, North Yorkshire,
England

British Library Cataloguing in Publication Data

Timperley, Rosemary
  That year at the office.—Large print ed.
  I. Title
  823'.914(F)   PR6070.I/

  ISBN 0-86009-581-9

First Published in Great Britain by Robert Hale Ltd, 1981

Copyright © 1981 by Rosemary Timperley

Published in Large Print 1984 by arrangement with Robert Hale Ltd,
London and Harvey Unna & Stephen Durbridge Ltd, London.

Photoset in Great Britain by
Dermar Phototypesetting Co., Long Preston, North Yorkshire.

Printed and Bound in Great Britain by
Redwood Burn Limited, Trowbridge.

'You cannot all of a sudden cease to be what you are: and you are what you have wanted to become.'

August Strindberg

CHAPTER 1

We were all in love that year at the office. It was as if the Great God Pan Himself had floated over us and cast His spell. We were not, I hasten to add, in love with each other, but with 'someone else'. But as we were all in the same state we found a certain companionship in our respective solitudes and sufferings. For love is such suffering...such a lonely business...

There were five of us in that section of the big office. It was an open-plan place, like an average school classroom when you come to think of it. A mass of people together, yet little cliques form in this corner or that. Those of a like mind get together. Yet often not deliberately together. Just by being physically placed together, a camaraderie arises.

We were friends who just happened all to be in love. Did we infect each other? Or is everyone always in love, unless very young or very old? And even then?

Anyway, it was as if the Pan-bomb had hit the five of us, so that, although we behaved fairly normally, inside ourselves we were shattered.

The five of us were Kate, Sam, Victoria, Rawden and I.

I was in the corner. Kate sat in front of me. She was a photographer, a slim red-haired girl who walked like an animal prowling through undergrowth, yet had the face of a pure-minded little angel. All the men found her a bit too attractive for comfort, but that has nothing to do with love.

Sam sat on my left. He did the 'Questions-and-Answers' column. What that man didn't already know he found in his own private filing-cabinet, full of newspaper cuttings and odd facts. He was a middle-aged Northcountryman who had never worked on a magazine before. He had come from Local Government, of all things; had started up his 'odd facts' business freelance, to make himself a bit of extra money—and the paper had offered him a staff job. It had seemed like a miracle to him. He was rescued from that world in which he'd been bored stiff and came to the magazine world, where he was no longer bored. He was 'doing his own thing' and being better paid for it than when he had been doing what his parents would have called a 'real job'. Poor Sam—if only he hadn't fallen in love...

Victoria, Vicky, sat in front of Sam. She did the film page. She was of Canadian origin. She was plump, rather plain if you count only physical features, but so full of comedy and character that really she was a charmer. Vicky was never afraid to be a clown. She was very emotional and very kind, but could be sharp with it—and she fell in love with the sort of monster known as 'a married man'. Love takes no consideration of propriety. It's wild.

Rawden sat in front of Vicky. He was Australian and had the accent to prove it. There was something a bit 'dumb' about him. A sort of stupidity, combined with cunning. Yet he was a pleasant enough chap to get on with. You'd have thought, however, that he'd be impervious to love. He was not. His job was that of

11

general reporter and feature-writer.

And I, in my corner, was the magazine's 'sob-sister'. Every day my desk was laden with tales of passion and of woe, of Puritanism and Porn, of Fetishism, Fanaticism, Fantasy and thoughts of *Felo de se*—intermingled with simple requests such as 'I have to be Best Man at a wedding. What do I *do?*' and 'I am a girl of fifteen and still don't know the Facts of Life—what are they—I daren't ask my mother' and—the most frequent letter of the lot—'I am a young man and I want a girl. How can I get to know one? I am very shy.'

If you get too empathetic with this sort of thing it can tear you to shreds. You feel with each letter and your own heart scatters drops of psychic blood. Then you grow hardened and it's all routine and you have a pile of stock replies and a secretary.

The fact that I, of all us five, had a secretary gave me a certain artificial prestige; although in fact my job would have been impossible without one, because of the hundreds of letters I had to send out, in their hopeful stamped addressed envelopes. Any 'broken heart' which didn't enclose an S.A.E. had no reply, unless I happened to be in a soppy mood and the letter rang a particular bell with me. Then I might answer. But I didn't have to. Anyway all the office routine was only background to my 'inner life'. For I was in love.

We were all in love! It was diabolical!

Kate, the red-haired photographer, was eating her heart out secretly over one of the reporters on the staff. He was dashing, fair-haired, very public school. Posh accent. Touch of a sneer to his lips. Sensitive behind all that. Idealistic. Kate saw through his pseudo-sophisticated facade and simply loved what she saw, behind the curtain of his pale blue eyes. Eyes full of pain. Unusual that. Most people with pale blue eyes are as cool as they look. He wasn't. His name was Andrew. His ancestors had come from the Hebrides. He hankered after mysterious roots which the public school had tried to deracinate. Hence his pain. And Kate, who was a bit of a glutton for punishment, couldn't resist another's pain. She wanted to *do* something about it. So she loved. Yet so quietly at first and thinking it was secret. But her eyes betrayed her. When she looked in his direction her eyes—changed. We all saw, we of the five. Our antennae were ultrasensitive because of our own inner state. Yet each of us thought his own heart was secret from the others, at first, before we began to open up with each other.

Sam was enamoured of someone completely beyond his range. Her unsuitability was obvious to anyone. But love takes no account of such matters. It plays jokes on people. The girl of Sam's daydreams, and probably night dreams, when he was cosily tucked up in bed with his wife, was very pretty and young. She was a new member of staff on the Woman's Page. The Woman's Page women worked in a separate room from the rest of us but it had glass walls, so we could see them, like goldfish in a bowl. Sam had to face that 'goldfish-bowl' all day. Every time he looked up he saw *her,* through the glass, lovely and silent, even when talking. She was a fashion and make-up expert and had been a model for a while. Even now I have never seen a prettier girl than Jonquil. That was her name and she *was* flower-like, albeit a painted flower. She made a work of art of her own already lovely face and poor old Sam fell, hook, line and sinker. Aside from her looks, however, she was not exceptional. Her mind was humdrum, her voice flat. But her figure was as exquisite as her face and she dressed attractively, as befitted her job—something different every day and always something which suited her. She was interested in her own career, even described herself as 'an ambitious girl'. Imagine someone saying, as she did, 'I'm an ambitious girl.' It makes you wince. But Sam winced only with agony and ecstasy. At the beginning I doubt whether it ever crossed Jonquil's mind that the middle-aged 'Questions-and-Answers' man on the other side of the glass adored her and observed her as worshipfully as a votary at a shrine.

The glass-walled room where the Woman's Page functioned was also the office library. We trotted in there from time to time to look up information, especially, in the case of the reporters, train times and so on. Sam was always going in there to look things up—things which he knew already—just for the awful joy of being nearer to his beloved. It was painful to watch him, knowing how he was feeling and seeing her complete indifference to him. Of course he was a 'married man', but love does not leave married men alone. It doesn't know about the rules of morality or if it does it doesn't care.

So there was Kate, secretly in love with Andrew, and Sam, secretly in love with Jonquil. Secretly? That's what they thought.

Vicky was 'secretly' in love with Tom. He was the chief photographer, Kate's 'boss'. He sat, oh anguish and delight! on Vicky's left, with only a gangway inbetween him and her. But because of the nature of his work he was seldom there. He would be on an outside job or in the studio or the dark-room. He stayed at his desk only when waiting for a new assignment. He and Vicky would chat together casually, but she was much shyer with him than with anyone else. She didn't clown and crack her jokes with him. He had no way of knowing how she felt. He was married anyway and had a daughter. He was older than Vicky, rather quiet by nature, as are most photographers—they live through their eyes and through their looking—and was, to my mind, a bit dull. Maybe that was why Vicky 'fell'. She was so very temperamental and his rock-like solidity was what she needed.

The love of Rawden's life was outside the office, thank goodness. None of us had met her. She was a Swedish girl called Ingrid and she and Rawden were living together. But she was in England for only a year, doing some training course or other, and apparently used Rawden as convenient lodgings, a sort of supper-and-sex arrangement. Nothing to do with love where Ingrid was concerned. So although Sam envied Rawden for living with the girl he loved Rawden was in fact worse off because of it. He had what he wanted—and yet he hadn't. Sam at least could still dream and hope for a miracle. For Rawden the miracle had happened and turned out to be straw and tinsel.

I, as much in love as any of them, was the mistress of a married man. It had been going on for years. It was all that deeply mattered to me. The rest was a performance. I never told the others about him because I was terrified that by a mere whisper of his name I might start a rumour flying; for although he didn't work on our paper he was in the world of journalism, where many people know many other people and exchange gossip between this paper and that. I knew that if anything happened to endanger his marriage he'd ditch me. I lived in daily dread of this coming to pass. Ridiculous? I know, but love is like that. It casts out reason and dignity.

It still strikes me as strange that we five should have been in this love-afflicted state simultaneously. For we had worked in a group for about a year without any such excitement and then it all happened at once.

Kate was the first to speak about her feelings. She came to her desk one morning looking excited. I studied her back view. It seemed to vibrate. Then she twisted round to me, as if she couldn't contain herself. 'I'm going out on a job this afternoon,' she said. 'A pub that's supposed to be haunted. I'm to take pictures and—and Andrew will be doing the interviewing.'

It was the first time she and Andrew had been assigned a job together. Usually Tom went with Andrew.

'How lovely for you,' I said.

'Lovely?' she said defensively.

'Well, isn't it?'

'Oh, Auntie, is it so obvious?' They all called me 'Auntie' because of my 'sob-sister' role.

'One can tell that you like him,' I said cautiously.

'Can you really? How awful!'

' "Love and a red nose can't be hid", Kate.'

She rubbed her pale little up-turned nose ruefully. 'Good thing I haven't got a red nose too. What do you think of Andrew?'

'I like him. He's sensitive.'

'Yes, he is, isn't he? He's awfully unhappy.'

'Well, I hope you have a happy afternoon together.'

'It won't mean anything to *him,*' she said sadly. 'Does this lipstick suit me?'

'Very well indeed.'

'Do I look better with eye make-up or without it?'

'With, if you do it carefully and don't just slosh it on, the way you sometimes do.'

'Yes, Auntie.' She grinned, like a little girl. Then she sighed and added, 'I don't know what's got into me, I really don't. After my husband, I swore to myself that I'd never bother about any man again.' Kate had had a divorce a couple of years back, mostly because her husband had found her too independent and un-domesticated, keener on her job than on him; so he had sought another woman more to his taste. Having married ideal-istically, believing in the 'for ever' bit at the time, Kate had felt that the ground was cut away from under her feet. A broken marriage is a dreadful shock to any woman, even, ironically, if she has ceased to care for the man himself—as Kate indeed had. It's not the loss of the chap that hurts so much as the loss of the dream; and the blow to self-esteem. Having promised to love for ever and then to stop loving, is a knock. You have broken your promise to *yourself*. You don't want to risk its ever happening again, but it does, of course.

She said now, 'It's the marriage promise that's wrong, isn't it? One shouldn't be encouraged to promise to love someone, when in fact you can't promise to have a certain feeling. You could promise to *do* this or that, but not to *feel* this or that. Yet they've cut out the "obey" bit, the one thing that you could carry out if you were determined, because it's doing, not feeling.'

'Yes,' I agreed. I had a broken marriage behind me too, although it was farther away in the past than Kate's. I was nearly forty and she was only in her late twenties, which seemed old to her but young to me.

After lunch that day Andrew came sauntering over to her desk. 'Ready for off, Kate? We're to get there just after lunch-hour closing-time and finish before they reopen at five-thirty. Honestly! Fancy being assigned to a pub job when it's closing-time! Just my luck!' Andrew tended to hit the bottle. His lunch had been several gins and a sausage-roll. He was rather flushed and had that 'unhappy' look which Kate couldn't resist. The 'little boy lost' expression.

When they'd gone Vicky turned to me and said: 'Lucky old Kate. The editor never sends me on a job with a man.'

'You're not a photographer,' I said.

'No.' She looked wistfully at Tom's empty desk. 'I don't know what's got into us lately, Auntie,' she said. 'There's poor old Sam having kittens over Jonquil and Kate making sheep's eyes at Andrew and Rawden going around looking like Hamlet because of his bloody Swede—and I've gone mad too!'

'Is that how you feel?'

'Oh, I don't know.' Her eyes were full of tears.

'At least you see him almost every day,' I said, for I saw the Love of my Life only once a fortnight, with luck.

'See who? Do you *know?*'

'Vicky, darling, you melt whenever you look at the chap.'

'Is it so obvious? Oh, how dreadful! He's out on a job this afternoon, so there's nothing to live for—yet it's a

22

relief too. I'm not sure which is worse, when he's there and I can't work properly for thinking of him; or when he's not and everything is empty and the minutes drag. It's like an illness.'

'It is an illness.'

'You'd say that, having all those "lonely hearts" pouring in every day. Are any of your correspondents as daft as me?'

'Most of them. It's life.'

Sam came along. 'So Kate's gone off with Andrew the Posh,' he said, 'She'll like that.' His heavy humour was trying, but he used it only to conceal his suffering. He had just been in the library and Jonquil had taken no notice of him at all. She'd carried on typing as if he wasn't there. His face was white.

Vicky went out then to interview a film actress for her page and Sam lingered by my desk. 'I'm in one devil of a mess, Auntie,' he said.

'Jonquil?'

'Now how on earth did you guess?'

'How did you "guess" about Kate and Andrew?'

'It sticks out a mile.'

'Yes.'

He flushed. 'Is everyone laughing behind my back?'

'No more than you were laughing at Kate just now.'

'I see. Except that I don't. I'm lost in a situation like this. I've never felt like it before. Never with my wife. I married her because I wanted to be married, to have a woman in the house, and we were good pals. We've hardly ever quarrelled over the ten years of our marriage. She's a good lass. But *this!*' He jerked his head towards the 'goldfish-bowl'. 'It's like being bewitched!'

'That's what it is. But do you mind?'

'No. No, I don't mind. I'd rather feel like this, in spite of the misery, than not feel it. What shall I *do?* If I invited her out do you think she'd come?'

'She might. If you made it very casual. A lunch-hour drink. We journalists often have lunch-hour drinks with each other. It needn't mean a thing.'

'I suppose I could have a lemonade or something.' Sam didn't drink alcohol. He went into pubs only when there was some sort of office 'do' and everyone went.

He'd gone redder than ever. 'Shall I go and ask her now?'

'Good heavens, no. That would make too much of it. Tomorrow, if she's in there before lunch, wander in to look something up, then ask her off-handedly if she's doing anything special for lunch and if she says "No" say: "Then how about a drink and a sandwich across the way?" '

'I'll do it,' he said. 'God, I shan't sleep tonight, thinking of it.' He was watching Jonquil through the glass. She smiled at one of her colleagues. 'When she smiles,' he said, 'I want to tear the pants off her.' Which was honest, if somewhat indelicate.

I felt rather guilty now, for 'encouraging' him, but when people want something very much I tend to help them towards it, out of an impulsive and thoughtless kind-heartedness. Then a harder, more sensible part of me perks up and says: You shouldn't have done that.

But he'd have gone ahead in some way or other, regardless of anything I said.

He was under a compulsion. As were we all.

Rawden was the next one to 'weep on my shoulder'. He lingered at six o'clock, when the others had left and I was signing my final batch of letters; for although I didn't have any more space in the paper than anyone else, I had more work to do because of the 'personal' stuff. Anyone who wanted to speak to me without the others being around simply hung about until shortly after six. I'd had some surprises in this respect too. One young man on the art staff, who had always put on an act of being most sophisticated and know-all—'a girl in every bedsit' image —crept up to me after office hours, made me swear I wouldn't tell a soul about his request, then admitted to me that he was still a virgin and as he was getting married in a month's time, and she was a virgin too, had I any of 'those little booklets which you send to your customers'? I gave him several, to read in bed before the fateful night, and he said: 'I'll probably have one under my pillow *on* the fateful night, in case I forget it all when the moment comes.' We laughed, of course, but in fact I was touched. It made me wonder how many other rather show-off young men are covering up their innocence.

Rawden, however, was a different kettle of fish. Sex-wise he was on the ball (if you'll pardon the expression), but love-wise he was a man in a maze. 'It's Ingrid, Auntie,' be began, in his Strine accent. 'She says she's going back to Stockholm at the end of the month and I don't know what to do. I've offered her every choice—to marry me and stay here —or to marry me and me go to Sweden with her—or anywhere else in he world— and for me to support her financially or not, as she wished—and to have kids or not, as she wished—but she says "No" to everything. What shall I say to her? How can I persuade her?'

It was so obvious, to everyone but Rawden himself, that he couldn't persuade her. That she was fed up with him. That she did not 'love him back'. And of course the more he went on at her, grovelled even, the farther away he drove her.

'I don't know what to do,' he went on.

'You know all about this sort of thing.' He indicated the letters.

'Just because I do this job doesn't make me know any more than anyone else,' I said.

'But you advise all these strangers.'

'Very rarely. The help they get is by writing their own problem down. By the time they've done that, they usually know what they're going to do. When I reply, I just make a few points then end up with "Only you can decide." '

'But I can't decide! Please advise me.'

'All right. Agree with her that it's best that you should part. Say that it's really quite a relief to you. That way at least you'll save your pride.'

'I have no pride left.'

'No doubt that's what she can't stand.'

He winced. Damn! The truth is always so cruel.

'You think I'm a bloody fool, don't you?' he said.

'No more than I am myself. Love makes fools of us. We know we should let go, more often than not, but we don't. We're afraid of the pain in store.'

'I think I'd kill myself if she leaves me.' And he rushed out.

Great help I'd been, I don't think! But there *is* no help, except what one can find within oneself, and if one can't find anything...I looked with misery at my telephone. Sometimes *he* rang me up. Today he hadn't. Each time the phone rang I nearly died. How I hated each caller who spoke in a voice other than *his*...Talk about 'Sob-sister cure thyself.'

So little I understood. So much cared. So unhappy I was. Yet I clung on to the situation as tenaciously as some of those heart-broken people who wrote to me. I could see what *they* should do, but I couldn't do it myself. When you're a professional shoulder to be wept on there is no shoulder for *you* to weep on.

In this black mood, I was just preparing to leave when my telephone rang. It was *him*. So glad he'd caught me before I left. Was I free tomorrow night? Was I! Angels sang. The world was a beautiful place. I loved him and I loved loving him and I had no regrets and what was wrong with the situation anyway? He gave me happiness, when he had time. What more could I ask?

I went home on air, the Great God Pan perched invisibly smiling on my shoulder, playing a few seductive unheard notes on his pipe. Oh, love was everything really and if you don't go after it with every bit of you you may as well not have been born.

Tonight was a happy night because he'd rung. Tomorrow would be a happy day because of the looking-forward time. Tomorrow night I'd wait in that little bar and he'd be late, as usual, but he'd come—and the pipes of Pan and the song of the angels would mingle and intermingle—and the day after that—

No. Face that when it comes and not before.

Tomorrow came. I was all inner world. I had to perform on the office stage until the evening. I would even enjoy it. I was confident and cheerful on such days, laughing at Sam's corny jokes which, on black days, made me wince; and what were Sam's corny jokes? They weren't exactly jokes. They were habits. If you arrived early at the office he'd say: 'Couldn't you sleep?' If you arrived late

30

he'd say: 'Good *afternoon!*' If you arrived exactly on time he'd say: 'Eh, on the dot!' You couldn't win—unless you laughed. And sometimes you couldn't laugh. And the fact that you knew he was a sad, sad man underneath all these would-be-humorous banalities didn't make you merciful in your feelings towards him—you just hated him—on black days.

But that day, when he said: 'Couldn't you sleep' when I walked in early, I said merely, 'Insomnia and I got wed long ago,' and he laughed. He was excited too. Of course! Today, in the lunch-hour, he was going to ask Jonquil out for a drink. His personal drama would come before mine. I had all the day to get through! But I didn't mind. I embarked on my letters with something almost like enthusiasm, dictated replies at great speed, then prepared my column for the coming deadline. When I'd finished it I knew it was quite a good one. I always worked best when I was going to meet *him* in the evening. So much he did for me, unaware. It's anticipatory happiness that counts most. You float on a rosy cloud.

When Kate came in and sat down in front of me I didn't take much notice. Then I remembered that yesterday had been *her* day. Had anything happened?

I wasn't left waiting long to know. She twisted round, beamed at me and whispered: 'Do you know, Auntie, Andrew has got a sword!'

At first, prurient-minded as I had become because of the correspondence I had to wade through, I thought she meant something sexual. I was even slightly shocked. But she meant it literally. After that first remark she told me that when they'd done their stuff at the 'haunted pub', which she and Andrew both thought privately was a gimmick on the part of the landlord, they'd had a drink at another pub and then she'd gone back with him to his flat for supper. And Andrew had an ancient sword hanging on the wall. It belonged to some wild Hebridean ancestor and he was immensely proud of it. As they were both rather drunk by that time, he had 'knighted' her with it.

'Then we went to bed,' she said. 'I

didn't go back to my own bed-sit at all. I stayed with him.'

So she had meant what I had at first thought she meant and yet she hadn't. Symbolism, symbolism all the way...

'Where is he this morning?' I asked, for Andrew's desk was empty.

'He thought it would be better if we didn't turn up at the same time. He's writing his article at home before he comes, then he'll just type it out when he gets here. I had to come to develop the pictures.' She dashed off to the dark-room.

She was so happy this morning, dear little Kate!

Vicky was less euphoric. She was plod-dingly typing out her interview with the film actress and getting the rest of her page together. 'Laugh, Clown, laugh!' she kept muttering. Tom was out on a job.

Rawden had not turned up at all. Had he murdered his indifferent Swede, or was he still in bed with her?

Come the lunch-hour, curiosity made me stay and watch how Sam got on. He'd been like a tom-cat on hot bricks all morning. Then the moment came. Jonquil was alone in the 'goldfish-bowl'. Sam went in there, to 'look something up'.

I watched the silent scene. Sam at the bookshelf. Jonquil typing. Then he spoke and she looked round. He gave a tortured smile. She gave a natural one. Had he invited her? Was she agreeing? Impossible to tell from this distance. Oh, go out with him—it means so much to him, I silently persuaded the girl. Suddenly she nodded and rose. Then she went off towards the washroom and Sam came pounding back to his desk. He collected some cash, which he kept in his desk-drawer in an old typewriter-ribbon tin—his secret cache. He looked at me and said:

'It worked. I'll love you for ever!'

And I wished suddenly, dreadfully, that it hadn't 'worked'. I saw tragedy... This wasn't funny at all. Ludicrous, but not funny. Like all passion. That girl was going to hurt him appallingly, without wishing to do so, and yet he was dashing forth, asking for the pain.

But I tossed off all worry about other people when I went out for lunch on my own. I had coffee and a sandwich at a snack-bar, then walked by the Thames and thought of *him*. The river was beautiful. Water flowing along always is, the shimmers and the ripples, the ever-changing reflections. I thought, When love is over and I have nothing left to live for, I'd still be all right as long as I could walk by a river, and see the sky. Then I thought of the thousands of people who can't walk, either by a river or anywhere else; and those who can't see the sky, either because they're blind or imprisoned. And I saw clearly that most of us simply don't appreciate our luck for most of the time.

Afternoon in the office was peaceful. Apparently Rawden had rung up to say he had flu, which, if it was true, would give him a release from mental anguish. There's nothing like bodily affliction to quieten the emotions. One becomes all physical self and to hell with the rest. Andrew arrived and sat at his desk, solemnly typing, not looking in Kate's direction. She, having developed her photographs, sat in blissful contemplation of a dream seemingly come true. Vicky was getting her 'copy' ready for next week's issue and was able to concentrate on it as Tom was not there. And Sam came back from his lunch-hour drink looking as if he'd been in paradise. He said nothing. He did no work. He just sat, dreaming. Just to be with her, he and she together, had filled his cup to the brim. For the moment he wanted nothing more. The only thing he said to me was: 'We went for a walk by the river afterwards. It was all so—' But he couldn't find a word.

I felt as if, in some strange way, my happy day was everyone else's too. I felt too confident. The hours passed slowly, but certainly. Soon I would see *him*. At five-thirty I went to the washroom to doll myself up for the great night. At five-forty-five I returned to my desk to sign my letters.

At five-fifty-five, my telephone rang.

He was there. He said he was 'terribly sorry, darling, but he couldn't make it tonight after all'.

'Really? Oh, well, never mind,' I said

and went on signing letters. It had happened before. It would happen again. Calm now. It doesn't matter. Don't let anyone see.

I myself couldn't see. Fiercely suppressed tears still kept welling up and half-blinding me. I didn't check the letters as well I should have done. I just scribbled my signature. Not that it was my signature. It was 'Auntie's', the name the office had given me for the job. I had three names: married name, 'maiden' name, office name. Who was I? Where was I going? Oh, please, someone—this pain—

But there was no one. There never is.

I suddenly thought of Rawden. That suicide threat. Had he meant it? Flu? Had that been the truth? The office had emptied out. Andrew and Kate had gone off together. Vicky had gone to a film première. Sam had gone home, to keep up some sort of an act before his wife—not that she wouldn't see through him like glass and know that something was up. I dialled the number of Rawden's flat.

There was no reply.

CHAPTER 2

I sat with the receiver in my hand, listening to the futile ringing. If he really had flu he'd hardly have gone out. If Ingrid had been there, looking after him, she would have answered the phone. If there was nothing she could do for him she might have gone out and he might be asleep or simply not want to bother answering phone-calls. Yet that was unlikely, for if Ingrid had gone out and then the phone had rung he'd have hoped it was her, checking that he was all right. People in love always answer the phone, unless the person they love happens to be with them at the time, then they may ignore the ringing. It was Rawden's mention of suicide and the fact that I'd been so little help to him that made me feel both anxious and guilty. Not that I'd have given Rawden a second thought if the Love of my Life hadn't let me down!

How about going to Rawden's flat and

seeing how he was? If I did and there was nothing wrong I might feel a fool, but it would be far worse if I didn't go and next morning we heard that he'd taken an overdose. It was just possible. Anyway, since selfish motives usually come uppermost, I needed something to *do*—something to give me a sense, or at least an illusion, of purpose.

I had never been to Rawden's place before, but I knew where it was, so made my way there quickly by Underground. I was still all dolled up as if for a date, but that wouldn't matter.

The flat was in a block. I found the number on the second floor, hesitated, then rang the bell.

There was no sound at all from inside. I rang a few more times then stood there helplessly. My suspicions were so fragile that I didn't want to go to the lengths of seeking out the caretaker. Maybe Rawden and Ingrid had simply gone out for the day and the 'flu' had been a lying excuse. Rawden was quite capable of that. But I wasn't *sure*. Suppose he was dying in there...

'Good-evening.' A voice behind me. A
39

woman's voice, charming, with that Greta Garbo quality, the sound coming somehow from the back of the throat. Before I ever heard other Swedish women speak I had thought that sort of voice belonged to Garbo alone, but they nearly all have it. So this was Ingrid. She had fair hair, a long, pale face and the sort of figure that men describe with their hands rather than with words and look as if they were caressing an invisible violin.

'Good-evening,' I said. 'I'm one of Rawden's office colleagues.'

'Auntie?' She gave it a funny little honking sound.

I laughed. 'Yes, that's right. We heard he'd gone down with flu and when I rang to see how he was there was no reply, so I came round—'

'I don't know anything about this,' she said. 'He was all right this morning. He set off to the office at the usual time. Looks as if he's been playing truant, doesn't it? I hope you won't give him away. Come in.' She unlocked the door and I followed her inside.

'Rawden?' she called. 'No. He's not back yet. I wonder what he's up to.' But she didn't sound as if she cared. 'Would you like some coffee, seeing you've come all this way?' she asked.

'Thank you. That's nice of you.'

'Perhaps you didn't expect me to be "nice" ', she said, rather mockingly, as she made the coffee. 'Rawden doesn't think I am, at the moment.'

'He's in love with you and you're going away.'

'It isn't my fault that he's in love with me. I'd much rather he wasn't. He's very difficult to live with at the moment.'

'Yet you came to live with him—'

'He wanted me to! I wish I hadn't now that he's become such a bore. A man should have more pride.'

'I can see it's not easy for you, but let him down as lightly as you can. Although he's travelled the world and had plenty of girls, I think you're the first one he's loved.'

'He is rather stupid and backward in some ways,' she said, 'but we had good times together before he became sentimental. You say he "loves" me, but it's such an uncomprehending love. If I loved someone I'd want them to be free and happy and do what *they* wanted—'

'He does want to do what you want, in a way.' I thought of Rawden's list of alternative courses of action.

'Only if he and I stay together and I don't want that. This has been an episode. Soon I'm going home. If I marry it will be to someone I can look up to, not down on.'

She had all the heartless honesty of one who has never been in love. She was being rational, which Rawden was incapable of being where she was concerned.

'Don't look so sorry for him,' she said, passing me a cup of excellent coffee. 'He's left girls who didn't want to be left. Now he's objecting to a dose of his own medicine.'

That was true too. Every cruel thing we ever do comes hitting back at us, sooner or later, and I could imagine Rawden being quite callous towards anyone he'd grown tired of.

Suddenly Ingrid said: 'Do *you* want him?'

'Me? Heavens, no!' But I could see why she thought it. I was wearing my 'party clothes' because I'd been expecting a night on the tiles myself, so it must seem to her that I'd come along to 'seduce' Rawden, catch him on the rebound, as it were. I decided to be open with her. 'I came because last night he told me you were leaving and he made a suicide threat. I didn't think he meant it, but I thought better be sure than sorry.'

She laughed. 'So when you rang the door-bell and there was no answer you imagined he might be in here with his head in the gas-oven—not that he'd do that as we have "natural" gas now. Very inconvenient for the suicidal. Rawden threatens suicide about twice a week, on average. "If you leave me," he says, "I will kill myself!" This is supposed to recommend him to me as a husband!'

'What do you say?'

'I tell him that his life is his own. What he does with it won't affect me one way or the other. I certainly wouldn't blame myself if he took his own life, but he won't. He uses the threat as emotional blackmail, that's all.'

'You don't seem worried that he's out now.'

'It's only eight o'clock. I expect he's

gone to one of those Earl's Court pubs where so many Australians hang out. He should go home too, back to his origins, marry a simple girl and rear sheep. He has an inexperienced soul.' She said this dreamily, as if in her own country men were made of nobler and more refined material. Europeans are still a bit snobbish about the Strines. It's their voices... they sound uncouth and slightly comic. But there was nothing comic about Rawden nowadays, unless one has a sick sense of humour. Maybe he was only 'a little boy who couldn't have his own way', but he was suffering from frustration and grief for all that. The flowers were not for him to pick...

I felt gloomy and full of foreboding when I returned alone to my flat. I set about undoing preparations I'd made for my lover's visit, then looked wistfully at the telephone. He wouldn't ring tonight. Obviously some important engagement had turned up, something to do with his wife. He'd be with her now. I'd never seen her, had no idea what she was like, except that once he'd said: 'She's a bit like you.' That made sense. Anyone who looks back on his lovers can see a basic similarity in them all. But this love business was a mystery to me. *Why* did one become an emotional slave to one person rather than another? It's much more then sexual attraction, although that is there, of course. Take Rawden and Ingrid. They had been sexually attracted to each other, but he was in love and she was not. Is it the lure of the unattainable then? As want means lack, obviously when you've got something you don't want it. But if you can't get it you go on wanting. Suppose the Love of my Life left his wife and came to live with me, would I still want him, after the novelty had worn off? Such self-questioning is very uncomfortable, for I had a feeling that if I had to live with anyone now I'd soon feel trapped and wish I were alone again. Solitude is bleak immediately after the break-up of a marriage, but unless you pair off again quickly you grow to like it. The selfish freedom of it is a precious luxury.

Next morning at the office Ingrid telephoned me. 'Is he there?' she asked.

'Rawden? No. Didn't he come home

last night?'

'He did not and he's never done that before.'

Again I thought of that suicide threat and my heart thudded unpleasantly. 'What are you going to do, Ingrid?'

'I'd better ring round to all the people we know, although there aren't many. Perhaps he's "teaching me a lesson". After all, as far as the office is concerned he's simply away sick. He won't know that you know that the flu was an excuse.'

'I suppose so.'

'Don't *you* worry,' she said. 'You have enough of other people's problems with that gruesome job you do. I only rang to see if he was there, not to bother you.' She rang off.

'What's up?' Sam asked. He was always curious about other people's telephone-calls—curious about everything, in fact. It was his trade to be curious, hence his 'Questions-and-Answers'.

There seemed no harm in informing him. He wasn't the sort to 'tell tales to the editor'. 'Rawden hasn't got flu at all,' I said. 'He's gone off somewhere. He didn't go home last night.'

'Was that his floozy on the phone?'

'It was Ingrid,' I said coldly.

'Well, good for Rawden,' said Sam. 'He's teaching her a lesson.'

'That's what she thinks too.'

'Plain as the nose on your face. That one's a proper little bitch if you ask me and old Rawden's getting his own back. More power to his elbow.'

'Oh, do stop talking in clichés, Sam.'

He turned away, snubbed. I'm the bitch, I thought. He means no harm. But he gets on my nerves. Five minutes later he got up, leaned over my desk and opened the window. 'Let's have some air,' he said. He often did this, without a by-your-leave, so that he could have some air floating across and I had a cold draught directly on me. If ever Sam and I had a real row, as distinct from occasional spats, it would be over that window. I'd have protested if I hadn't previously been so rude to him. As it was, I said nothing and put up with the draught. I did, however, rather conspicuously pull my jacket over my shoulders, but I doubt whether he noticed. He was goldfish-bowl watching now and his face had become so vulnerable in the space of a second that my irritation died away. He'd evidently forgotten my sharpness too, for he turned to me and said softly: 'Why *her* and not someone else?'

'She's extremely pretty,' I said.

'Mmm.' He pondered this, as if it were a deep thought. 'Mmm. I suppose if she had a face like the back of a bus and a figure that was once round me and twice round the gasworks I'd not have looked at her twice.'

'You wouldn't have looked at her once, old mate,' I said.

We laughed, then got on with our work.

I studied the next letter on the pile. It read: 'I am a woman of thirty-five and am having an affair with a married man. He does not love me as I love him, only uses me as a convenience.'

Yes, they really do write things like that, in all solemnity. And it's not funny. The giggle it evokes is hysterical.

'Sometimes, when we have a date, he puts me off at a moment's notice, because his wife wants him for something. I'm sick to death of playing second fiddle—but I really do love him, so what shall I do?'

What will you do, you poor little soul? You'll go on and on putting up with it. I know. What *should* you do? You should tell him to go to hell and find a 'convenience' elsewhere...

And what would I reply? Something on the lines of: 'Dear Miss X, Thank you very much for your letter. I do understand how unhappy you are, but no one can really advise you over a matter like this. You know yourself that it would be sensible to break the affair now, but it's because you find yourself unable to be "sensible" that you wrote. Perhaps one day soon you will meet someone else who can take this man's place in your life—' and so on and so forth. And if the recipient of my answer already had the 'someone else' glimmering on her horizon she'd think: That's a good reply. She *knows*. But if there was no 'someone else' and she was as deeply sunk in the ooze as I myself was she'd think: Silly old cow! Understands nothing! She might even write and say so.

I remember one young male correspondent who wrote: 'A year ago you gave me some advice on a love affair. I took your advice but it all went wrong. Now I have another love affair on my hands and am going to give you another chance. My problem is...'

They were so funny—and so touching.

The next letter was rather pathetic porn. The young man described an incident in his life, or that was what he said it was, but in fact I'd read it a number of times from different senders. They get these pornographic books, you see, then copy out passages which appeal to them, then copy them out again in the form of a letter and pretend that they themselves are faced with this particular situation. This was the story of a man with a beautiful young wife who has men going in and out of her bedroom all day, and he has to sit and watch. No detail is spared in the description of what goes on. This letter ended: 'Seeing that I still love my wife, what should I do?'

My instinct was to reply; 'Read better books in future,' but I always had to 'Play safe', not show my scepticism—

'Never mock your readers!' was the editor's instruction, 'For in them lies our bloody circulation.' Playing safe would be a brief note: 'Dear Mr X., Thank you very much for your letter. You will have to decide this complicated problem for yourself.' I longed to add: 'Why not tell it to the marines?' but never did.

The next letter awakened instant suspicion in me, for it started off: 'I am an O.A.P.'

Now there's absolutely nothing wrong with being an Old Age Pensioner. It happens to us all at sixty or sixty-five, if we are unfortunate enough to live so long. A sixty-five-years-old millionaire will be an O.A.P., if he paid his contributions—that is a big IF I know—he probably never paid anything state-wise at all, but fled the country in terror of having to part with a penny towards the welfare of others—but you get the point. Anyone who starts off a letter: 'I am an O.A.P.' wishes to create a picture in one's mind of some pathetic, poverty-stricken creature, with his gas and electricity cut off, no more than a loaf of bread in his cupboard, rats in the skirting and an avaricious landlord pounding on his door and asking for MORE. There are many O.A.P's who do live like that, I'm sure, but they're not the sort to write and if they ever did they would not start off 'I am an O.A.P.'

This one went on: 'I have fought in two wars for my Country and it treats me rotten. I can't stand these Blacks and these Jews and all these other forreners. They are invading our green and pleasant land. I dare you to print this letter!'

Poor old b. Little did he know that hundreds of correspondents end their letters with exactly the same 'challenge' and if we printed them all there'd be no room for anything else...no Woman's Page, no film page, no 'Questions-and-Answers' and, horror of horrors, no pin-ups! It was the pin-ups that, basically, sold the magazine.

Thinking of pin-ups, I glanced across at Tom's desk. He was there. This was his pin-up day, when he was not sent on outside jobs. He sweated in the office studio instead, turning a girl into a seductive picture for the front page. He had many artificial aids. There were mock-busts to fix to the flat-chested, wigs for the scanty-haired and all sorts of weird and wonderful garments which showed a bit here and a bit there. Tom's pin-up pictures were more seductive than any nude, which hides nothing. 'It's the bits you *don't* see that count,' he said once. 'You have to suggest the way but never get there—better to travel hopefully and all that jazz.' It was the love-of-the-unattainable syndrome brought down to basics. Tom's other artificial aids in the pin-up realm were provided by the toucher-up. He could fine down a pudgy waistline, enlarge eyes, slenderise necks and calves. Once he'd slenderised a model's large feet so enthusiastically that in the following week we'd had shoals of letters asking why the front page pin-up had only eight toes instead of the conventional ten?

Tom, at this moment, was going through a pile of pin-up photographs with the serious concentration of one studying Sanskrit or Chinese. Vicky called across to him:

'How do you know which one to pick?'

He didn't even look up. He said, 'I go by the eyes.'

This was what made him good at the job. You can always get the pin-up's body right, by this means or that, but a girl with hard, calculating eyes makes a bad pin-up. She has to have innocent eyes. That was what made La Monroe the Living Pin-up.

'I think you're wonderful the way you do it,' Vicky mumured and Sam cast a glance in my direction, as if to say: Another victim. Then he resumed his goldfish-bowl-watching. He'd been at it for an hour now...

My telephone rang. Oh, God, let it please be *him*...I lifted the receiver. A voice began immediately: 'Are you the one what does the advice column?'

'I am.'

'Then I think you are a—' It went on for some seconds. Then I rang off. I never grew completely hardened to those calls. All very well for the psychiatrists to say that the callers are 'disturbed' and need sympathy. I felt no sympathy. I was merely sickened, as when one steps into a mess of dog-shit. More so, because a dog has to shit and it's not his fault if no one has trained him—and yet, and yet, I suppose the same can be said of people who make such telephone calls. No one would wish to behave so vilely, so there must be compulsion at work.

'What was that?' Sam asked, intrigued by the telephone call, no doubt noticing my nauseated expression.

'Only a customer telling me what he thought of me, mostly in four-letter words.'

'You shouldn't have to listen to that sort of muck.' He pronounced it to rhyme with 'book'.

'Part of the job,' I said.

'What did he say exactly?' An avid expression in Sam's eyes.

I just shook my head. There was a part of Sam that not only understood but envied the caller.

Towards the end of the afternoon Rawden drifted in. I was so relieved to see him! But he looked ghastly. His face was grey and he had great shadows under his rather snake-like eyes.

Vicky said: 'Rawden! You shouldn't have come in with the flu! You look like death warmed up. Anyway, we don't want to catch it.'

'*You've* caught it already,' said Rawden. Unrequited love had actually made him enigmatic. He sat at his desk, not to work, but rather like someone coming home after a long day and resting in his chair. I suppose the office was the only place where he could relax. If he had stayed out to punish Ingrid he had punished himself far more. Hoping to cheer him up, even if only a little, I went and whispered in his ear: 'Ingrid rang. She was anxious about you.' He reddened and looked at me with tortured eyes. 'Where have you been?' I asked.

'Nowhere,' he answered.

Sam was watching us. I wished I hadn't told him about Rawden now. It wasn't his business. If only he wouldn't listen in to my phone calls all the time. He very rarely received any himself, that was the trouble. The only ones he didn't ask me about were the rare ones from the Love of my Life. Sam *knew* and would put on a face of studied unhearing. That showed some consideration, I suppose, but oh he was a pest. I longed for his holidays...

Holidays was a subject that came up just before going-home time. From May until the beginning of October there was always somebody away, so our group of five altered in character, becoming an ever-changing foursome. Now Vicky stated that she would be on holiday next week and the week after. She was going to Switzerland, she said glumly. We all said how marvellous that would be, but knew quite well that she was dreading it: a whole fortnight without even *seeing* Tom! Oh, yes, time is so long, so very long, when the loved one is out of sight but will not go out of mind. Sam would be dreading his holiday too. Two weeks without so much as a glimpse of the fair Jonquil, let alone the ecstasy of a lunch-hour drink and a walk by the river afterwards; two wife-filled weeks would be bread-and-butter-pudding every day for Sam, never a sundae with a cherry on top. Kate might have been dreading her holiday but for the fact that she and Andrew had at last got together and, although she said nothing, I could tell by her face that they would be trying to have the same two weeks. Kate had changed even in twenty-four hours. She had blossomed. Fulfilled love is a great beautifier, a flame which sends out its radiance. But a flame also clings to the object it burns. The object cannot throw it off. It takes an outside force to stamp it out or drown it and when that happens the radiance of the fire is gone and what remains is charred, shrivelled and unlovely to look upon. God—why was I having such morbid thoughts about Kate, the only happy one of us five? I suppose I merely saw through Andrew in a way that she did not. He was sensitive about himself and enamoured of her at the moment, but he was only using her really. He was only a man...See how clearly I saw where others were concerned and how blindly I went on along my own narrow tunnel to nowhere.

Now Vicky was saying to Tom: 'Shall you miss me when I'm away?'

'Of course I shall, Vick,' he said politely, gathering his pin-ups together and going to the editor's office to present the chosen one for the Old Man's 'okay'.

'Englishmen are so passionate and

58

romantic, are they not?' Vicky said mockingly, adding, in rather good imitation of Eartha Kitt: 'A Canadian needs aidin', Hm! But an Englishsman needs *time.*'

We laughed and Sam said: 'You should be on the stage.'

'I am,' said Vicky. 'I'm never bloody off it!'

Then Sam and Vicky left at the same moment, clattering down the back stairs together, because it was quicker than going out by the front, and Kate and Andrew eyed each other across the room. He gave a small jerk of his head which probably meant 'the pub across the way in five minutes' and left on his own.

Kate wheeled right round on her chair, making it swivel, so that she was facing me. 'Andrew and I are going to try to have a holiday together,' she said, 'but we've got our names down for different fortnights. We've looked at the holiday schedule and, Auntie—darling Auntie— you're down for the same fortnight in June as he is. Have you made plans? Or would you do a swop with me? My fortnight is in July. I know it's an awful nerve to ask, but would it make any difference to you?'

'Not a bit,' I said immediately. 'I don't care when I have my time off.'

'You hadn't arranged to go anywhere with—er—anyone?'

'No. Let's go and alter the schedule now,' I said, 'then when you meet Andrew you can tell him it's fixed.'

'You're an angel! Would you like to come over and have a drink with us? On the house, as a "thank you"?'

'No, thanks, love. I have things to do.'

It was a lie but I saw her relief. Just to be *à deux* with Andrew was still elixir of the gods to her, after such a long time of longing.

The holiday schedule was pinned to the notice-board. The arrangement was that we had to fill in our three-week periods, a fortnight plus a single week, and it was first come, first served. Too many staff must not be away at the same time. After the first filling-in, exchanges went on, such as Kate and I were carrying out. And I saw something pathetic. Vicky's fortnight, beginning next week, had coincided with Tom's. She had done that so that when she was away he would be too, so she wouldn't be 'missing' anything. But Tom had apparently had a change of mind, for he had swopped with someone else, so his fortnight was now in August. The best laid schemes...

Kate noticed this too. She pointed to the alteration and said: 'Hard cheese on poor old Vicky,' I nodded, but my heart sank as I observed something else. My new fortnight in July coincided with Sam's, so I would no longer have the luxury of Sam's desk empty beside me for two successive weeks. How trivial such things are and yet they affect one. Damn Kate and her love life, I thought in a moment of uncharity.

When I returned to my desk and Kate had gone, my letters were waiting to be signed. The office had almost emptied out, but Rawden still sat there droopingly.

'How worried did she sound?' he asked me.

'Ingrid? She wondered where you were, naturally. What did you do, Rawden? You look really rough.'

'I went to a pub and got drunk, then I

walked about all night. I mingled with the down-and-outs and felt like one of them.'

'But why did you stay away from the office yesterday?'

'I don't know really. I just suddenly couldn't face it, so I rang to say I'd got flu. I think I have now too.' He paused, then asked: 'Why did she ring *you?*'

The truth will out. Ingrid would tell him I'd called, so I'd better mention it. I did. He wanted to know if we had talked about him and what she had said. I told him, missing out the unkind bits. 'You'll have to settle for it, Rawden. The girl's going home to resume her former life-style. Her year in London has been a separate thing. Try to understand. You should. You've ''loved and left'' people yourself.'

'That's no consolation,' he said.

'Go home now anyway and rest up—and stop the suicide threats. They cut no ice with Ingrid.'

'Ingrid,' he said bitterly, 'is made of ice.'

'Maybe that's why you love her—the lure of the Snow Queen.'

'Do you mind!' he said, giving me a look which I no doubt deserved and he shuffled away. He really was a bit wet! I didn't envy Ingrid tonight.

Whom then did I envy? The Love of my Life's spouse? Not really. Presumably if I'd been the spouse she or someone like her would have been the 'bit on the side'. I wondered if all 'bits on the side' loved their men as I loved mine. Mine. But he wasn't. He wasn't anyone's. He was his own. To say of any other person 'He, or she, is mine' is a pathetic lie.

One of my correspondents had written today, of her errant husband: 'I can't bear to lose him. He's all I've got.' I should have replied honestly, 'Madam, no one has *got* anyone, ever,' instead of handing out kindly platitudes.

Being a 'sob-sister' is not an honest job.

Still, it pays well and I'd rather do it than clean public lavatories. The women who do that for a pittance are heroines unsung. Especially one dear old thing who looked after the LADIES at Bank Underground. She probably isn't there now, but she used to keep the place so neat and sweet and bring flowers, paid for out of her own wages. There *are* good people in the world...

My letters were ready. The office boy came to collect them for the post. He was a sparky, larky kid and, when he picked up the pile, pretended that it was immensely heavy and staggered under the 'weight'. 'Cor, Auntie,' he said, 'I can't take all these at once. I'll have to take them one at a time.'

'Would they feel lighter if I bribed you with a fag?'

'Well! That's funny!' He straightened up. 'They're light as a feather already.' I gave him his fag, which he put behind his ear. 'You smoke a lot, don't you?' he said.

'I'm afraid I do.'

'Nerves, I s'pose.'

'Idiocy more like. It costs a bomb and it's bad for you.'

He lingered still. He'd gone serious all of a sudden. 'Can I ask you something?'

'What is it, Dave?'

'If you were a girl of, say, fifteen, and a boy asked you out to the cinema and

took you home afterwards—a first date
—would you expect him to kiss you?'

'When I was fifteen I was such a drab,
shy little thing that no boy asked me out.'

'But if he had would you 'ave?'

'No, I don't think so, but times have
changed. Anyway, it depends on the girl.
Some would expect a kiss, some
wouldn't I suggest you play it by ear.'

'Who said anything about me?' he
protested. 'I was only talking theoretical.' He marched off. I called out:
'Dave!' He stopped and turned, looking
such a child, pink of face and with the
jaunty cigarette behind his ear. 'Give her
a great big kiss if *you* feel like it,' I said.
'If *you* feel right about it, then it'll be
okay with her—touching wood, of
course.'

He grinned, shook a threatening fist at
me, then left.

It's little things like that which keep
one going.

My telephone rang. *Him.* 'Ah, I've
caught you!' You have indeed, in a steel
trap...'Hello, darling,' I said. 'Yes, I was
just about to leave.' He was so sorry
about last night. How about Friday? It

would have to be Friday or nothing as he was going on holiday with his family for three weeks, starting next Monday. A proud woman would have said, 'Then let's make it nothing, shall we?' A woman in love says what I said: 'Friday will be lovely. I shall long for it.' I was so very attainable. I was even grateful that he could spare me part of his precious Friday. Of course, he could always ring again and cancel it. Bitter thoughts spoiling happy anticipation. Then the fact of the blank three weeks after the Friday sank in. How would I get through them? Oh, God, make it stop...

Suddenly the editor came out of his room. 'Ah! I'm glad I've caught you,' he said. 'Will you come into my office for a minute?' He was looking grim.

I forgot all about love on the instant. I was a child summoned to the headmaster's sanctum.

What had I done?

CHAPTER 3

'I have warned you time and time again that you must be careful when you reply to readers,' he began. 'Look at this.'

He passed me a typewritten letter.

'Dear Sir,

'I am writing to you, the editor, to complain about one of your staff. I found a letter which your advice columnist had written to my wife. In it she makes a defamatory statement about myself, when she knows nothing whatever about me and knows only my wife's story. I demand an instant apology and you are fortunate that I do not take the matter to court. If I do not receive an apology, however, I *will* go to court.'

There followed the writer's backward-sloping signature, a neurotic 'fist' if ever there was one.

'What did you say in your letter?' the editor demanded.

'I can't remember off-hand, Mr

Hargon, but I'll fetch the wife's letter and a carbon copy of my reply.'

'Do that.'

I hurried to the big filing-cabinet in the outer office and, thank goodness, found the letter easily. At least my filing-system worked and my secretary was doing her job properly. I recalled the letter as soon as I looked at it. The woman said her husband knocked her about and I, cowardly and aware of the danger of interfering in such matters, had written what I thought was a sympathetic yet cautious reply. My caution had not gone far enough. I had dictated the fatal sentence: 'I am so sorry that your husband is unkind to you.' Really, I must be slipping. The rule was that my replies be worded so that it wouldn't matter into whose hands my letter fell. What I should have put was: 'I am so sorry that you are unhappy over this matter.' That could mean anything. She might have been writing to say that her bust was too small or she could never get her sponge-cakes to rise or that her telly had gone wrong...anything. As it was...

I took the original letter and carbon

copy of reply to the editor. Immediately he stabbed at the carbon. ' "I am so sorry that your husband is unkind to you!" You should never write "your husband" anyway. "He" is good enough. I'd have thought you'd been at this job long enough to know—'

'I'm very sorry,' I said. 'A stupid mistake. I'll write an apology, of course.'

'First thing tomorrow, and bring it to me before you send it. I'll have to write too.'

Absurdly, I felt tearful. As a schoolgirl I used to almost cry when I was ticked off and now, at nearly forty, the sensation was the same. Be your age, I told myself.

Then Hargon surprised me. In a quite different tone he said: 'I expect you find it galling never being able to write straight-forwardly to these people. This woman's letter strikes me as a true one and the husband must be a bit of a bastard. Still, this is popular journalism, not social work. We're here to sell the paper, not mend broken lives. All right?' He smiled a little. 'Off you go—but don't do it again or I'll have your guts for garters!'

'I won't. Good-night, Mr Hargon.'

The Old Man wasn't so bad. All the same I was 'properly shook up' and retreated into one of the cubicles in the washroom to have a swift and private weep. I cried far too easily, not over big things, but over small, unexpected ones. People in love are like that, when they are not loved back enough. But what was I drizzling about? I had Friday evening to look forward to. Only tomorrow to get through, then it would be Friday. Oh, my darling, when I look at you in my mind's eye, I regret nothing at all...

When I came out of the cubicle, recovered, I found to my surprise that someone else had come in. The fair Jonquil, no less.

'Hello, you're late,' I said.

She pulled a little face and said: 'I'm waiting for someone outside to go away.'

'Someone pestering you?'

'Not exactly pestering, but he waits to "see me to the station".'

'Who is he? Discarded boyfriend who won't let go?'

'Actually,' she said, standing before the mirror and repainting her flower-

70

mouth, 'it's Sam.'

'But Sam went home ages ago!'

'He pretends to, but he comes back.'

'How long has he been doing this?'

'Only the last couple of nights. I suppose I was a bit stupid really. I had a drink with him in the lunch-hour, day before yesterday, and in the evening he was waiting outside—and again yesterday evening—and he's sure to be waiting there tonight. It gives me the creeps!' As she had been speaking I noticed, for the first time, a trace of north-country accent.

'Do you come from the North yourself?' I asked.

'Yes. It's in my voice still, is it? I've tried so hard to get rid of it. Elocution lessons and all that. I'm an ambitious girl, you see. It's no use having a northern accent in London unless you're an actress or a man.'

That was shrewd enough.

She was 'doing' her eyes now and most effectively. The child knew all about make-up.

'You're not afraid of Sam, are you?'

'Well, I am a bit. I don't know what

71

he's after. I mean, he's old enough to be my father. I liked him at first because he reminded me of Dad and Dad's so far away. He asked me out for a drink and only drank lemonade himself—just like Dad—and we went for a walk by the river. It was nice. I like being with older people once in a while. But now—Oh, I don't know.' Her face was finished. She studied it earnestly in the glass, as if she were examining a picture she had painted —as indeed she was.

'Have you a date tonight?' I asked, thinking of my own fragile attempts at glamour when I had a date with *him*.

'No,' she said. 'I don't bother with boys. It's my career that matters to me.'

Her 'career'. The pathos of it! Working on the Woman's Page of this crummy paper. And yet—it's difficult enough to get a job on any paper at all, especially in London. Everyone starts small. Maybe one day her ladyship would be editing *Vogue*. Stranger things have happened in this utterly strange world.

But I saw that the flower-like Jonquil was hard as nails at the moment. She was over twenty, but still had the imperviousness of childhood. No one had feelings but she. The rest was a backcloth against which she played her part. It was a nuisance when a human being, such as Sam, got in the way.

'Would you do something for me?' she said.

'Within reason.'

She laughed. 'It's easy enough. You're leaving now, are you?'

'I am.'

'Then can we go together and talk to each other and pretend not to see him? I'll be safe once I get to the Underground. I've got my "Season" and can dash straight down the escalator.'

'It's raining,' I said, seeing and hearing the tap-tapping rain against the frosted glass of the windows.

'Oh, good,' said Jonquil. 'That'll make it easier.'

'Won't it spoil your make-up?'

'Not really. There's a way of keeping your head down so rain doesn't hit your face and I've got a scarf.' She tied a scarf over her head. It was quite shocking that someone who looked so beautiful should

73

be so banal.

'Right,' I said, 'we'll go out together.'

We went out together, into the rain. From the corner of my eye I saw a waiting shadow, a gleam of adoring eyes. And I felt like a Judas. Sam was my friend, not Jonquil. Sam, of the corny jokes and the window-opening. Sam, who loved.

'Thanks ever so much,' said Jonquil, when we reached the Underground and she went striding youthfully down the escalator to the lower depths. I followed more slowly, feeling a heel. Poor old Sam. Standing there in the rain. What excuse did he make to his wife for arriving home later than usual? 'Traffic holup' probably. Useful things, traffic hold-ups. The perfect excuse for a man with a dream...

But next morning at the office Sam looked down-in-the-mouth. He must have been feeling really bad, for when I arrived five minutes late, he didn't say: 'Good *afternoon.*' What was wrong? His morning greetings, with their predictability, drove me round the twist—but, when there was no morning greeting,

74

instead of being thankful, I felt upset. However, no time for upsetness this morning. I had to get my letter of apology done and take it to the editor. I'd written it out in rough at home and now typed it myself, rather than bothering my secretary. Then I took it to the Old Man. 'What's this?' he said, frowning. He was knee-deep in page-proofs.

'The letter of apology you wanted me to write to—'

'Oh, yes, yes, I'd forgotten. Leave it there. And tell Tom to come in here, will you? I'm not so sure about this front page pin-up after all. Her hair's too straight.' I left him scowling at the long, lank hair of the otherwise glorious model, innocent eyes an' all. Some men are never satisfied!

I passed on the message to Tom, who said: 'Her hair? We can easily put a few kinks in it if he wants it wavy. I don't know, I really don't!' It's a weary, weary life for a pin-up photographer. Vicky followed him mooningly with her gaze, then saw me looking at her and made dramatic gestures of adoration, such as kids make when they mention their favourite pop stars. 'Laugh, Clown, laugh!' she said, in a broken voice. Bless her, she did laugh at herself. She was always on the edge of laughter or tears— yet she could be most businesslike when she was out on the job. She had the ability to put her personal passions aside when she went to interview people or collect film information. She ran her page efficiently and wrote it with wit. She could have found a job on a better paper than ours, but never tried for one as it would mean 'leaving Tom'. More people let their careers be influenced by such matters than they will ever admit and it's not only women who are so 'silly'. Men do it too, but cover up better.

Rawden had arrived. He still looked ill but was working on an article and had that don't-anyone-speak-to-me air. His typewriter had a frantic sound. I've noticed before that the sound of a typewriter often shows the typist's mood. Gaiety or gloom comes over through the tap-tapping. I wonder if one can also tell if a woodpecker is in a happy mood or not...

Kate was busy in the dark-room, so

Sam could speak to me without her over-hearing. He said: 'You saw me last night, didn't you?'

'Last night?'

'Come off it. You both swept by as if I were a bad smell. Was it chance that you were together or not?'

'Sheer chance. We happened to be leaving at the same time.'

'Why so late?'

'The Old Man "kept me in after school" because I'd made a hash of one of my letters.'

'But why was *she* late?'

'Sam, what is this? An inquisition?'

'She was deliberately avoiding me, wasn't she?'

'Oh, you are an old masochist.'

'I'm losing all ways,' he said. 'I had one hell of a do with my wife last night.'

'A row?'

'Not exactly. We never row. But when I arrived home late, soaked through, she said she knew something was wrong and wouldn't I tell her what it was. Well, how could I? You don't *tell* your wife that you care for someone else instead of her. "Is there another woman?" she asked and she made it sound as as if I'd been having it off with some tart. Had I been "unfaithful"? Well, I denied it till I was black in the face. Trouble is that although I haven't been "unfaithful" in the technical sense, that's only from lack of opportunity, so I felt as if I was lying even though I wasn't. It's a right bugger.' (He pronounced this to rhyme with 'sugar').

I said nothing but looked sympathetic.

'You must think I'm a bloody fool,' he said.

'We all are at some time or other, Sam. I'm amazed you've never been through anything like this before.'

'I must be a late developer,' he said wrily. 'But I did feel like this once before. I'd forgotten, but it came back to me last night, when I couldn't sleep. It was when I was still at school and I used to see a girl from another school, on the bus. I only spoke to her a couple of times. She'd have no truck with me. It was anguish. And now it's happening again.'

'Sam, don't wait outside the office for her in the evenings. She doesn't like it and if it's upsetting your wife too—'

'How do you know she doesn't like it? So you and she did leave together on purpose. I guessed as much. But what have I done to annoy her? It doesn't seem much to ask, just to walk along to the station with someone in the evening.'

'She's very young.'

'All right, you needn't dig it in. Do you think if I asked her out for a drink in the lunch-hour today she'd come?' He went on quickly, before I could answer. 'I'll do it anyway. I must find out what she's suddenly got against me, when I've done nothing. I haven't even made a pass!' Somehow his cosy northern accent made all this sound even more pathetic.

Accents in speech have more effect than one is always conscious of and we five had such a variety of them. Vicky's Canadian drawl would make her sound casual and cynical when she wasn't necessarily feeling it. Rawden's Australian vowel sounds caused him to seem stupider than he was. Kate spoke clearly, without any special accent or affectation: the voice of the well-educated English girl, but not public school educated—no 'plums in the mouth'. It used to be called 'received pronunciation' by the educationalists, or 'R.P.' for short. I myself spoke 'R.P.', or hoped I did. I probably had a few echoes of my childhood Cockney floating around. But of course as soon as I say that Kate spoke 'without any special accent' I betray my own narrowness. Vicky would have said Kate had a 'very English accent' and regard her own tones as 'without accent'. As far as Sam was concerned, Kate and I 'talked posh' and Vicky and Rawden 'talked American'. He called Andrew either 'Andrew the Posh' or 'Lord Muck' (to rhyme with 'hook'). Dave, the office boy, was broad Cockney and did bad imitations of Sam's Northern speech— until I ticked him off once and told him that he might remedy his own speech before he started jeering at other people's. He had been rather shaken, obviously regarding his own accent as normal and correct English. The truth is that we all think our own accents are normal and correct and everyone else is peculiar.

Sam went into the 'goldfish-bowl'

before lunch and I saw him speak to Jonquil. She smiled but shook her head. Their lips moved. Sam reddened, then came back to his desk. He began to type furiously. He was still typing when I went out to lunch.

When I came back I was in time to see him place a letter on Jonquil's desk and my heart sank. If he'd written her a 'love letter' she'd be appalled. He sat tensely, waiting for her to return. When she didn't come immediately he dashed out to the washroom and Kate, who had also watched this pantomime, looked round at me and pulled a face.

By the time Jonquil did come back we five were at our desks and all knew that Sam had written Jonquil a letter. We watched her, as if she were an actress in a silent film. Two other women were in the 'bowl', the Woman's Page editor, an overpainted, overdressed and bejewelled middle-aged woman, who always wore a hat in the office—God knows why; and her anxious, plump and frumpy secretary. These two were working together and took no notice of Jonquil, who sat down, looking lovely as ever, and drew a

81

file of papers towards her. Then she saw the letter. She opened and read it. She sat perfectly still for a second, as if making up her mind what to do, then she deliberately tore it into pieces and dropped it into the waste-paper-basket. She knew he was watching, the little devil, but she didn't look through the glass in his direction. He had gone deathly white. He rose and went out to the washroom again.

'The little cow!' said Vicky. 'Oh, poor Sam!'

'He was a fool to write it,' said Kate.

'Hear, hear,' said Rawden. 'He should have more pride.'

'Look who's talking,' I snapped.

'No one in this corner of the office has any pride,' said Vicky, in exaggeratedly tragic tones. ' "Starve, scourge, deride me, I am dumb, I keep my secret still!" '

' "Fools! But I also had my day!" ' Kate continued.

'Oh, we all know about *you*,' said Vicky. 'You're a thoroughly immoral woman.'

'What were you quoting, Vick?' Rawden asked.

'Chesterton's *The Donkey,* you ignorant Pom.'

'I thought that was a religious poem,' said Rawden.

'Love is a religious subject,' said Kate, 'Isn't it, Auntie?'

'Yes,' I said. For when we fall in love with a person, we are really falling in love with God, whom we glimpse, for incomprehensible reasons, in this person or that. Not that knowing this with one's mind makes the slightest difference when emotion takes over. Today will soon be over. Tomorrow will be Friday. Oh, my darling...If you cancel our date again I'll kill you!

Sam returned. He was green in the face. 'I've got the most frightful headache,' he said, 'and I've just been sick as a dog. I'll have to go home. Tell the Old Man if he asks for me.'

'Oh, Sam!' Vicky came over to him, all concern. 'Shall you be all right? Shall I come with you?'

'No, thanks, Vicky. My wife would have a fit. She's suspicious enough as it is.'

'Shall I ring for a taxi for you?' I suggested.

'Eh, that's not a bad idea. At least if I'm sick again in the taxi there'll only be the driver and me to see the mess. I'll go and wait outside. Tell him to stop at the back entrance.'

'I will, Sam. Take care of yourself.'

I ordered the taxi and that was that. Saddened, we all got down to work and hardly spoke for the rest of the afternoon.

Later I noticed something. At five-thirty, when the other Woman's-Page-women had gone, Jonquil went over to the waste-paper-basket and retrieved some pieces of paper. Not difficult to guess what they were. But why was she rescuing the letter? Vanity? Sentiment?

She came over to me after the people who sat around me had left and I was signing my letters.

'I need your advice,' she said. 'Look at what Sam wrote to me while I was out at lunch.'

She placed the pieces of the torn letter before me and fitted them together. It was typed and began: 'My dearest Jonquil—' I put my hand over it.

'Look, this is a personal letter from

him to you. I don't want to read it, Jonquil.'

'Please do,' she said. 'If there's any trouble, I want someone here to know what I'm up against.'

'Aren't you making a fuss about nothing? The poor man's gone home sick. Migraine, by the look of him. You're not "up against" anything, you silly girl.'

'Please read it,' she said. 'There's no one I can turn to. I've no close friends, my relations are miles away and I can't go to Mrs Bellen' (that was the Woman's Page editor) 'because she doesn't really like me.'

That did not surprise me. Mrs Bellen couldn't possibly like someone so pretty. She desired to be 'fairest of them all' and Jonquil, who had been appointed by Hargon, not her, must be a thorn in her ageing flesh; especially when the girl was competent and she could find no reason to complain of her.

So, although I felt disloyal to Sam, I read the fragmented letter: 'My dearest Jonquil, If I have done anything to offend you, please tell me what it is, then

I can make amends. Your company gives me more happiness than I have ever known and when you are not there, I think of you all the time. You are the most beautiful girl I have ever seen. I would do anything in the world for you. You have only to say the word. I would never have the courage to say this to you, because although people think me brash and talkative, I am really very shy— when I am with someone I care deeply about. I care about you, my darling. I love you. Sam.'

It was a child's letter: that 'shadow' side of him which had never grown up, because it had been kept hidden in a cellar of the unconscious. It knew nothing of reason and convention. It discarded propriety. It was all primitive desire. No wonder he'd been sick and had a blinding headache. He was being split in two...

'I think he's gone mad,' said Jonquil. 'Don't you? I mean, he's an old man and he doesn't even know me really.'

'People often fall in love with unsuitable people,' I said mildly. 'In fact, it's more the rule than the exception.'

'But what shall I *do?* It's so awkward with us being in the same office. He glares at me through the glass all day, making it difficult for me to work, and my work matters to me.'

'You'll just have to freeze him off, Jonquil. I expect you've had practice in doing that to men. You're very attractive.'

'I know I am, but I'm not common. I don't go around "asking for it" the way some London girls do. If I'd led him on I'd say it was my own fault—but this isn't.'

'No, it isn't. There's no question of fault. These things happen.'

'You're not being much help,' she said.

'I didn't want to read the letter in the first place. It's personal and private. He'd hate it if he knew I'd read it.'

'Then maybe if you tell him you've read it he'll feel ashamed and leave me alone.'

'Oh, let it ride for the moment,' I said, tired of the whole business. 'If he's as ill tomorrow as he was this afternoon he probably won't come in, then there's the weekend.'

'I don't think you're taking it seriously enough,' said Jonquil. 'It's a *mad* letter to get from a man of his age. He might do anything.'

'He would never do anything to hurt you, that's for sure.'

'Well, I'm not so sure! I thought you'd be more understanding, I must say.' She picked up her bits of letter and moved away. Her parting shot was: 'You're willing enough to help a lot of strangers but when I bring you a real problem you just say: "These things happen." You're a bit of a fraud—Auntie.'

And in my heart I could not but agree with her. The truth was that I felt no spontaneous affection or affinity towards the girl. I hoped I wasn't jealous or her youth and looks, as Mrs Bellen was. It's so difficult to know oneself. Just now she had seemed a cool little bitch, yet she was only trying to protect herself from anything that might cause trouble at the office, wherein lay her life's ambition...

'Letters ready?'

'Oh, Dave, you startled me. Hang on,

I haven't finished signing them.'

'You were miles away,' he said. As I signed he continued: 'I took your advice.'

'What advice?'

'*You* know.'

'Oh, yes. The great big kiss. It was all right?'

'She lapped it up,' said Dave.

'You'll be asking for one of my "little booklets" next.'

'Me?' said Dave, with arrogant male contempt. 'They couldn't tell me nothing!'

Amazing what a response to 'a great big kiss' can do to a boy.

He went off with my letters, whistling *Raindrops are falling on my head*. I felt as if raindrops were falling on mine too, although the office was dry as a bone and empty as a skeleton. I couldn't get the Sam-and-Jonquil saga out of my mind. This time tomorrow night, my darling, I shall be getting ready for seeing you—all tomorrow daytime to get through—time so slow—I need a drink!

I didn't often go into the pub across the way by myself, but tonight I did and

the first people I saw in there were Kate
and Andrew. They were talking and
drinking together, seriously yet lightly.
They radiated happiness.

This was the sunny side of the street of
love.

How long would it last? Oh, never
mind about things' lasting. Nothing does
anyway. Not even life.

Kate looked across. 'Auntie!'

I didn't really want to be the 'goose-
berry', joining them, but I had no choice.
I went over. 'Hello, you two.'

'We owe you a drink,' said Andrew,
'for swopping holidays with Kate the
way you did. It was extremely good of
you. What shall it be?'

I had wanted a quiet vodka, all by
myself, but this was not to be. 'Thank
you, Andrew. Vodka, with a little water,
would be lovely.'

'You look worn out,' said Kate, while
Andrew was at the bar counter. 'The
"lonely hearts" getting you down?'

'No more than usual.'

'I wonder if Sam got home all right,'
she said.

'He would. Trust the London taxi-driver.'

'He's an awful fool, getting hooked on that little twit.' Kate was arrogant in her happiness. She had forgotten what an 'awful fool' she herself had been now that, by chance, things had turned out right for her.

Andrew returned with my drink and refills for himself and Kate. 'Cheers,' he said. We 'cheered' back.

'Have you decided where to go for your holiday?' I asked, making conversation to 'pay' for my free vodka.

'We thought, a cottage somewhere,' said Kate.

'A touch of the old primitive, back to the land and all that,' laughed Andrew, seriously.

'As a matter of fact,' said Kate, 'the Old Man has a cottage. He lets it out sometimes, if he's feeling *simpatico,* or so Andrew says.'

'I'm going to sound him out,' said Andrew. To me, he sounded like a con-man. Kate looked at him with unguarded love.

Poor little devil, I thought. And then: But I expect this is how *I* look at *him.*

What fools love makes of us! It's not fair!

All's fair in love and war.

And the one can so quickly change into the other.

The pendulum swings.

We talked trivially for a while. The robot which takes charge of me in times of stress worked well, mechanically. The moment came for the robot to rise, say a graceful 'thank you' and 'good-night' to the loving couple and then depart into its solitude, lit with searchlights of hope because tomorrow night *would* come—it needed only time to get there...

And suddenly Rawden walked in.

He moved like a zombie and made straight for the bar counter. He ordered a double Scotch. Usually Rawden drank beer, complaining the while that it wasn't as good as Strine beer.

Kate called: 'Rawden!'

He turned. He stared. He lifted the whisky to his lips and drank it right down.

'Is anything the matter?' I said feebly.

'Nothing at all,' said Rawden. 'Ingrid has left me. Nothing is the matter.

Nothing is left. I am on my way to the top of a high building. I shall jump off it. I thought I needed some Dutch courage first.'

He threw his emptied glass across the bar. It fell with a crash. Glass flew. He ran out of the door like a madman.

Andrew, Kate and I followed.

CHAPTER 4

We lost him. The streets were dark and there are many alleyways in that area.

We stood in a dismayed triangle and looked round at the nothingness and the nobody.

'Do you think he meant it?' Kate gasped.

'Oh, he meant it,' said Andrew. 'I've said things like that and meant it. It doesn't mean one does it. And thank God one didn't.' He put his arm round Kate's shoulders. They kissed.

'There's nothing we can do,' I said. 'Go home, you two.'

And they went, just like that. I found myself standing alone in the small, dark street, looking this way and that, peering up at possible buildings which might make a jumping-off ground for a suicide. Our own office building was the obvious one. For a start, Rawden would be able to get inside, if he spun a yarn to the night doorman, who would know him by sight as one of the reporters. I hurried to the front entrance and rang the bell. The old doorman came, sleepy-eyed, a small, strong cigarette between his lips. 'Oh, it's you, dear,' he said. 'You forgotten something too?'

'Why? Has someone else been here?'

'Yes. One of the blokes. Left his brief-case here, he said. He's gone up to "editorial" to collect it.'

'I've left some papers I want to work on. May I go up?'

'Certainly, Miss.'

I walked up soundlessly on the car-peted stairs instead of using the lift. It was unusual for me to come in by the front. As my corner desk was nearer to what we called the 'back door dive', I normally used those stone stairs which always reminded me of the back stairs of cinemas. Incidentally, only the editorial staff were allowed to use the front entrance when coming to work. The men who did the real work, the compositors and machine men, had to use the back entrance. This was a curious remnant of social snobbery which shocked me so much that at first I hadn't believed it. But it was true. A skilful and experienced compositor must use the back entrance, but any silly little copy-typist who happened to work in 'editorial' might use the front, the posh entrance. These apparently trivial things are far more responsible for industrial friction than the so-called 'important issues'.

Now I reached the editorial floor, pushed open the swing doors and looked across the big office. Empty desks, covered typewriters and crouching telephones looked like strange animals in some stone-still jungle. They had a waiting air, menacing almost. In the small hours, of course, the place would come alive with cleaning-women, those heroic souls who worked there every day, just as we did, but we never met each other. It would be possible for, say, a cleaner and a reporter to work in the building for twenty years and their paths never cross. Two different worlds playing Box and Cox with each other. Occasionally a cleaner would 'come to life' by leaving a note on some one's desk, such as: 'Pleese do not stamp yore fag-ends into the floor. Theres ashtrays int there?' or, 'Will you put yore torn up paper in the wast paper basket insted of scatering it about like confutti.' If I'd been a cleaning-woman I'd have *hated* us messy lot!

Now, feeling afraid, I walked right across the office and out to the back stairs. There I walked up instead of down. Again, I had rarely walked up those stairs to the departments above our head...departments full of machinery and ferocious-looking men. But all was silence there tonight. On and on, up and up to the roof. In summer staff sometimes sunbathed on the roof during the lunch-hour. I'd been up once myself, but was repelled by the unlovely bodies spread out on the grey ground. Sunbathers always *look* so awful, don't they? Especially the men, proud of their hairy chest or showing off their shoulder-muscles. From childhood onwards I have always found men more attractive with their clothes on—even the Love of my Life looked more beguiling dressed than undressed—although I'd have died sooner than tell him so.

My head was full of these foolish, whirling thoughts, as if I were trying to calm my fears by thinking only of trivial things. Did I really imagine that Rawden would be here and about to jump off the roof? No, not really—and yet—

Cold wind. Night sky. No sign of any-one. I walked to the edge and looked over. Deserted street. Then a voice behind me, startling me so much that I nearly toppled to my doom—

'What are *you* doing here, Auntie?'

I came back from that fateful edge. Rawden was leaning against a chimney-stack, so firmly flattened against it that he'd been all but invisible.

'I came to find you,' I said. 'Come down with me, Rawden.'

'I was going to jump off.'

'Why? To "get your own back" on

her?'

'I've got nothing to live for!'

'Oh, my dear child—' I went over and put my arms round him. I hadn't really thought it would be any use, but it was. He suddenly collapsed against my shoulder and wept. He *was* only a child. He had travelled across the world and visited a number of different countries, had done a variety of jobs and 'laid' a variety of women, but none of it had reached *him,* the way love does. He was a little boy alone in the foreign country of his own heart. Now I guided him, as if he were a patient and I a nurse, down the stone stairs and into our corner of the office. I sat him down on his own desk. He began to recover. I gave him a cigarette and had one myself.

'Tell Auntie all about it,' I said.

'She's gone home. When I got back to the flat this evening all her things had disappeared and she'd left this note.' He handed me a scruffy little note which looked as if he had been crushing it in his fingers for a long time. I smoothed it out and read: 'Dear Rawden, I am cutting my stay in London short and going home now. I didn't tell you as I could not face a lot of argument. We have not been happy together lately, have we? Forgive me if I am hurting you, and thank you for your hospitality. You will get over it sooner than you think and find another girl. Sincerely, Ingrid.'

'I'm so sorry, Rawden,' I said. 'It's hell for you. But at least it's over now. It's this business of waiting for her to go and trying to persuade her not to that's been driving you crazy. Now, it's finished and you *will* get over it.'

'It's easy to talk,' he said.

Yes, indeed.

'Excuse me—' The doorman's voice from the distant doorway.

'We're just coming,' I said. 'I found my old mate here and we started gossiping.'

The doorman gave us a canny look, suspecting a rendezvous.

'Find your brief-case?' he asked Rawden.

'No. I must have left it somewhere else.'

'But I found my papers,' I said, collecting some from my desk drawer, just for show. Then the old man ushered us out and locked up behind us.

'I'll see you home,' I said to Rawden.

'You needn't. I'll be okay now. I'm just tired. Thanks for everything. Don't tell the others about tonight.'

'I won't, my dear. Good-night.'

And I watched the lonely Australian walk away.

God, what an evening! I felt tired out myself. Oh, well, tomorrow evening will come and there will be a shining time and its light will have to last me for three whole weeks afterwards. Rawden had no such tomorrow to look forward to. He would wake to the dark. And one day it will be me. It comes to us all. Love is a fearful thing!

Friday daytime was peaceful. Rawden came, looking white and shadowy, but was sent out on a reporting job straight away. Sam's wife rang to say he was in bed with migraine, so the desk next to mine was empty. Kate and Andrew were given another job together and off they went, full of the joys of spring. Vicky was working very hard, as she had to provide enough material to cover her holiday period. That was the worst of doing a regular column. Before your leave you had to work like stink to cover the 'missing weeks' and when you returned there was a backlog waiting to be attended to. The reporters and photographers were luckier in that respect.

But it was a good thing that Vicky was so busy; it stopped her from brooding. At five-thirty Tom left, with a casual wave of the hand and, 'Have a good holiday, Vick!'

'Thank you, Tom. I shall,' she said sweetly, then sat for a moment, quite limp and still, letting the pain wash over her. Then she was tap-tap-tapping again and went on till six o'clock.

'Finished!' she announced at last. 'All ready for the Old Man. God, I'm beat! I haven't even done my packing yet. Come and have a drink with me, Auntie.'

'I can't tonight, Vicky. I have to—' As I spoke, my telephone rang. And I knew before I answered. I knew. I lifted the receiver. *He* was terribly sorry—he wouldn't have had it happen for the world—but as he was going away on Monday there was a whole pile of work to get through at the office and he simply couldn't make our date after all—it was impossible—

You're impossible, my thoughts screamed. I hate you!

'Never mind,' I said, aware of Vicky's listening face. 'It's not your fault. Have a good holiday. 'Bye.' I rang off and turned to her with a smile. 'I can have a drink with you tonight after all. Good idea.'

'Laugh, Clown, laugh?' said Vicky. She knew. We all knew about each other now. We were all so sorry for each other. It was all so silly—yet so deathly serious.

In the pub, over our drinks, gin for Vicky and vodka for me—weren't we fortunate to be able to afford such luxury?—I asked, 'Are you going alone to Switzerland?'

'Sure. If you can't be with the one you want it's better alone.'

'Yes.'

'You're lucky,' she said. 'At least yours comes to you sometimes. Tom doesn't even know I care, or if he does he's not letting on. And that's not just because he's married. Look at Sam. He doesn't let a little thing like a wife stop him from going after what he wants. He's a fool, but you can't help admiring him, in a way.'

'He'll make himself ill if he's not careful.'

'We're all ill in Heartbreak Corner. It's like a plague. Kate's on top of the world at the moment, but that won't last. I know Andrew's type. He's shallow. Kate is deep. She *feels*. Keep an eye on her, Auntie. We're a bit like a family in our corner, aren't we? We get on each other's nerves with our habits and peculiarities, but there's a bond. I shall miss you all when I'm yodelling alone on a Swiss hill-top.'

'Two weeks isn't long.'

'It will seem long,' said Vicky. 'Shall I send him a postcard?'

'I don't see why not.'

'I will then. I'll send postcards to you all. I wonder if they have any of those gorgeous vulgar ones over there, great big fat women and little droopy men with walrus moustaches. I'd like to find one with a girl making goo-goo eyes at a handsome hunk of man, offering him a little white flower and saying: "I bring you idle-vice!" Still, it would be no use sending anything pin-uppish to Tom. He gets such an overdose. Maybe that's what I'm doing wrong! Do I dress too sexily?'

Vicky did dress rather sexily. She went in for tight shirts and plunge necklines. As I made no comment, she went on: 'I'll change my image when I come back. I'll try to look ladylike, like you.'

'Heaven forbid!' I said and we laughed together. Yet we were so wretched in our different ways. I was trying to stop myself from thinking about what tonight should have been— the shining time. When I got home I would probably start having a long, bitter conversation with *him* in my head. I might even mutter some of my passionate speeches aloud. This was beneficial, incidentally, as I got it out of my system, then when I did meet him I could be sweet as pie. *When* I did meet him? Don't I mean *if?* Two cancelled dates in one week, then a three weeks' break. It looked suspiciously like a gradual brush-off. 'You *will* get over it,'

I'd said to Rawden and he: 'It's easy to talk.'

'You,' said Vicky, 'have gone into a long black daydream.'

'I'm sorry, Vicky. How rude of me. One for the road?'

'No, thanks. I have to go and pack. I must also develop a stiff upper lip.' She drew her top lip down over her teeth and muttered: 'The honour of the regiment, doncherknow!'

She was laughing as she left, with tears in her eyes.

I stayed alone and went on drinking. I began to dramatise myself a little, as if I were the love-crossed heroine of one of those romantic films one saw in the thirties and forties. Many a time had my dear Bette Davis sat lonely in a bar, being so effectively tragic that there wasn't a dry eye in the house. How I had loved the cinema in those days! I was all set for a series of tragic love affairs when I grew up. I wanted them! Well, I got them all right. But self-dramatisation is no consolation when you actually are 'crossed in love'. The suffering is too damned real. And humiliating. Careful. I'd soon be dropping maudlin tears into my vodka. Get up and go, you silly fool. I got up and went, aware that I had to think about each step I took as the carpet kept waving up and down. I made it to the Underground, however, and stood on the escalator, clinging to the handrail. When I reached the platform, zig-zagging slightly, I had forgotten all about my broken heart and was simply concentrating on not disgracing myself in public. A woman of my age, getting drunk! Really! I should know my limits by now. But it was all *his* fault. *He* was driving me to drink...and so on...

By the time I had swayed carefully home my drunkenness was diminishing. Wearily I unmade the preparations for the evening that should have been, then, stabbed by hunger, ate bread and cheese and drank black coffee. I was about to go to bed when the door-bell rang. Rawden? Needing help? I hurried to the door.

A woman was standing there, a stranger.

'I've come for my husband,' she said.

CHAPTER 5

'There are no husbands here. Who are you?' I said.

'I'm his wife and I know he's here.'

I shook my head. 'Come in and look for yourself.'

So this was his wife. She was about my age, well-dressed, and extremely fraught. Her face had that frozen look of one who is taking desperate measures. She looked round the flat, saw the remnants of my solitary supper, then said: 'He was coming here tonight. I know it. I've known for a long time when he's meeting you. I can tell by his face in the morning, the way he says: "I may be late tonight. I'm having a few drinks with the boys." Where is he then?'

I saw no point in fencing with her.

'He's working late,' I said. 'A pile-up of jobs in preparation for his going away. You're off on Monday, I believe.'

She nodded. 'Yes, and I wanted to get

this business settled first. I hoped to find you together and make him choose.'

'He'd choose you. There's no question of anything else. I'm not a home-wrecker.'

'You've wrecked our home!'

'Have I?' I was genuinely surprised.

'Well, what do you think?' she blazed. 'How do you imagine I feel when he crawls home after being with you, and telling me a lot of lies?'

'He doesn't know. Men are very young. Please sit down.' She sat. 'Would you like some coffee? I'll make some more anyway.'

My drunkenness had worn off now as if it had never been. I was thinking fast. I decided to be straight with her. I gave her a cup of coffee and a cigarette.

'You must have felt pretty desperate to come here like this,' I said.

'I am.' She sipped her coffee, inhaled nicotine.

'Why? You know him. If it wasn't me, it'd be someone else. Men need *more*. It doesn't mean they're displeased with what they've got already. Just that they need *more*. I'm only his "bit on the side''. The fact that I love him makes it safer for him. He knows I'd never hurt him, in any way. Least of all to harm his family life. That's his anchor.'

'I'm getting tired of being a bloody anchor!' said his wife.

And how I sympathised. This was no enemy. It was a kind of *alter ego*. I said: 'I'd feel the same in your place.'

'But you're not in my place, are you? Oh, this is turning out all wrong—I wanted to find you here together and—and—'

'And make your ultimatum? Her or me?'

'Yes!'

'That was brave.'

'I'm not brave, but determined.'

'You love him so much?'

'It's nothing to do with what you call ''love'',' she said. 'He's *my* husband.'

'If you didn't love him you wouldn't care a pin what he did in his spare time. In fact you might be quite relieved to have him out of the way.'

'You're different from what I expected,' she said.

'You expected someone beautiful and

glamorous, and young perhaps? And you find an ordinary woman, rather like yourself.'

'In a way,' she admitted, then blazed up again: 'You've got to let him go! He's mine!'

'I don't think you need worry,' I said. 'He's going off me already. I've seen the signs. He cancelled our last date and he cancelled tonight. I think his excuse was genuine, that he really was "Kept late at the office", but a man who's head-over-heels in love chucks the office and goes after the desired one. I am no longer the desired one. I think he's getting rid of me, gently-gently, trying not to hurt me—doing it in his own good time. You know how kind he is.'

'Deceitful!' she said.

'Kindness is always deceitful. Only the cruel are honest.'

There was a grim silence, then I asked, conversationally, 'Where are you going for your holiday?'

'Italy. Rome, Florence, Venice. A week in each place.'

My envy rose up like a black mountain. God, to go to those places with *him!*

What was this woman complaining about?

I said: 'Then what on earth are you doing here? If you love him, you have three weeks of heaven in front of you! You should be thanking God!'

'Don't you talk to me about God,' she said, 'When you obviously have no morals or standards whatsoever. Does he pay you?'

How she hated me. But then, come to think of it, I'm not all that fond of myself...I see myself through her eyes.

'No,' I said coldly. 'I earn my own living. As far as I can make out, he spends everything he earns on supporting you and your house and your children. In fact if money ever comes into things I lend it to him, when he runs short. His anchor is rather an extravagant one. When I say "lend" I don't expect to be paid back. It's a term we use.'

'So *you* pay *him* for his "services",' said his wife.

It was becoming really nasty now, Strindberg *à la carte*. We were no longer 'two ordinary women'. We were witches. Women are so, when they get together and go down to basics. Compassion flies out of the window, even if the window is closed, and an evil spirit enters the air—through that same closed window. Was that why Sam always wanted windows open, because he knew that closed ones encouraged strange devils...

'Stop this,' I said, pulling us both up. 'We're going a bit wild.' I tried to think of her now as someone who had written to me on the 'sob-sister' column. What would I say to her?

I said: 'You're going to have three weeks with him in Italy. Make the most of it. Be kind to him and let him be kind to you. Forget all about me. *He* will. And now, please go.'

I felt numb when the other woman had gone. Other woman? I was the 'other woman', she the 'wife'. Labels, labels... This numbness. What had happened hadn't really sunk in yet. I had not absorbed it into myself. It was hovering outside. I suppose I was simply suffering from shock. There was no pain. Nothing seemed to matter.

Then the telephone rang and hope brought pain. Please God let it be him—I can tell him about tonight—warn him—

I grabbed the little black animal that was the telephone receiver. My hand was sweaty. 'Hello.'

'Sam here.' A distant, whispering voice. 'I've only got a minute. My wife's having a bath. Was she in the office today?'

'Your wife?'

'No, no—her.'

'You mean Jonquil? Yes, she came to work as usual.'

'Did she say anything?'

'What about?'

'Don't fence with me. Just tell me. You knew I'd left her a letter. I'm afraid now that it might have made things worse—that she'll be angry—'

'Oh, Sam, be your age. What does it matter if she is angry? She's only a chit of a girl. She's not a patch on you when it comes to—to kindness and human feelings.'

'So she is angry. She told you. Did she show you my letter?'

It was no use keeping things from him. 'She showed it to me yesterday evening. I didn't want to read it, but she insisted.

She was quite upset and, Sam, you really mustn't go on with this. It was all right when she saw you as a sort of father-figure, but as a suitor—well—'

'I'm quite prepared to be a father-figure if that's what she wants,' he said eagerly. 'I'd never touch her if she didn't want me to, any more than a father would.'

'But she'd know you were wanting to all the time. Don't you see? You've got to check your desire for her before it grows any stronger.'

'I don't think it could,' he said. 'Nothing else in the world matters to me. I'd chuck everything and go away with her, if she'd have me. Oh, blast, my wife's coming.' He rang off sharply. And I'd forgotten to ask if his headache was better...

But what a state everyone is in. Why are we all being afflicted like this, all of a sudden, out of the blue, as if, as Vicky suggested, we were infected by some plague? The plague of love. There was Rawden, full of death-wish and going about like a zombie; Vicky probably weeping over her packing at this very moment; Sam frantic with frustration and migraine; Kate—she was happy now, too happy for safety—the pendulum was swinging too far in one direction—it would come zooming back one day and I, the woman in the corner, driven right into the corner, helpless and frightened and refusing to admit to myself that my love affair was over and it was likely that I would never see *him* again. His wife would see to that. She wouldn't let him have his cake and eat it. I looked at the weekend before me and wondered how I was going to travel through it. Every day, from now on, would be such a long journey.

The telephone rang again. I answered without hope, expecting Sam again or Rawden.

'Darling?' he said. And angels sang.

'Oh, darling, hello!'

He had just rung up to say good-night and repeat how sorry he was. He would miss me while he was away, and so on.

'It's very sweet of you to ring. Thank you,' I said, then, as the angels stopped singing, I took a deep breath and went on: 'It's a good thing you didn't come here tonight. Your wife turned up—to catch us *in corpore* whatnot.'

'She *what!*'

I told him much of what had been said, not all.

Poor man. He was so horrified it was almost funny. Tragedy was tipping over into farce. To my horror I heard laughter creeping into my voice.

'I'm glad you find it so amusing,' he said.

'I don't really—I don't—'

'You see what it means?'

'What?'

'It means that I shan't be able to see you again, not now.'

'I see. And shall you mind very much?'

'Of course I shall mind! It's part of my life!'

I nearly said: It's *all* of my life. But that would have been a bit too corny, even coming from me; although it *was* all of my life that mattered to me then. It was my inner life. How would the outer life carry on without anything inside it? Would the hollowness show?

We were both still hanging on to the

telephone, not knowing what to say next. He did mind a little—of course he did— and he'd mind more later, for when something is gone we start wanting it. It was one thing to keep putting me off when he knew I was always available, but quite another to give up coming here entirely because his wife wouldn't stand for it.

He said, 'You see that I have no choice, don't you?'

'Yes.'

'I'm terribly sorry, darling! It's something I've always dreaded. I've no idea how she found out. I've been so careful. Oh, this is awful! I'd hoped to enjoy my holiday too.'

'You'll still enjoy it. Be the repentant sinner and put on the old charm.'

'You don't sound like you when you speak like that.'

'Really? Under this saccharine surface there is a core of iron. Didn't you know?'

'Oh, please,' he said. 'I'm unhappy too.'

And that made me cry, damn and blast it. Messy tears sopping down my face. Thank goodness it wasn't a picturephone!

'I still love you,' I gasped, all pride forgot, then I rang off quickly, ashamed of the tears in my voice. Stupid hysterical female! No wonder men use and despise us. Why can't I be hard and indifferent like—like whom? I couldn't think of anyone. I didn't count Jonquil. She had the young coldness of one who has not yet been reached, but one day she would be. Nobody else of my acquaintance was really hard and indifferent. I don't believe anyone is. Some people pretend to be, to protect themselves, that's all. And that was what I would have to do myself. I must keep the outside shell in good condition. It must not collapse merely because it was empty. A fearful stillness came over me. A little death. Worse than the marriage break-up. I had never loved my husband as much as I loved *him*.

The weekend passed very slowly. I kept looking at the clock to see how time was getting on and it went at such a snail's pace that I thought there must be something wrong with the clock's mechanism. I checked the time with the radio again and again, only to find that the radio was 'going slow' also. It was really grim. I was glad to go to work on Monday morning. Letters from the 'lonely hearts' would take my mind off my own.

It was a funny old Monday. Vicky's desk was empty and I missed her brightness. Sam and Rawden both looked like death warmed up. Kate was in a dream and her eyes had that still-in-bed look. And my letters were thoroughly nasty.

When you run an advice column certain subjects come in waves. One week it seems as if most of the female population is worrying about being pregnant and unmarried; another week there's a flood of 'unfaithful husbands'; another, 'unfaithful wives'; another, it's all girls asking how they can fatten up their bust-line, and another, how they can slim down their waistline. This Monday there was a burst of what I called 'spanking letters', i.e. topic of flagellation. The correspondents write to say how much they enjoy spanking or being spanked and go into great detail. It's all part of the job and there's none so queer as folks, but it leaves a nasty taste in the mouth. On this particular Black Monday I could have done without it. The only small 'silver lining' was that it cheered Sam up. He was fascinated by what he called 'filthy letters' and I let him read some, although I shouldn't have done. Not that I think the perverts would have minded this 'lack of confidentiality'. They're exhibitionist to a man, or woman. There were some other fetishist letters too—the rubber sheet syndrome and the tight corsets kink. When I'd first started being an 'Auntie' I had thought in my innocence that these letters were hoaxes, people trying to be funny. But they meant it! And there were hundreds of them. It's an Underworld and sometimes its inhabitants perk up and write to the press. The fact that it comes in waves is still a mystery to me.

My secretary took a more cheerful attitude. 'Oh, goody,' she said, 'lots of dirty letters means most of them are anonymous so we shan't have to reply!'

But I'd wanted a *busy* day, to take my mind of *me*. As it was, I finished dictating unusually early and it was too early in the week to get my column ready. Time was going slow again.

'You're looking down in the mouth,' said Sam.

'These letters are enough to give anyone the pip.'

'Let's have some air.' He opened the window above my head. The cold draught blew down on me. I didn't care.

Morning coffee came and Sam took some pills with his.

'Headache looming up again?' I asked him.

'It's there all the time, just nagging, but nothing like as bad as it was on Thursday and Friday. I nearly died.' He added, 'She hasn't looked at me once.'

'Stop looking at *her,* you silly clot.'

'I can't,' he said. 'She's like a magnet to my eyes.'

Later he went into the library and gazed at books on the shelves. Jonquil did not turn her head.

Kate said: 'I wish Sam would pull himself together. It's getting embarrassing. I hate watching a man make a fool of himself.'

'He can't help it. Don't you be so

smug.'

'Oh, Auntie, I'm not!' Then she whispered: 'I'm happy!' and gave me the most beautiful smile. It scared me. The happy are so vulnerable once they admit their happiness. It's tempting Fate.

Same came back to his desk and, with a grim expression, dialled an internal number on his phone. A second later I saw Jonquil pick up her phone. Sam said quietly: 'Why did you ignore me when I spoke to you just now? What have I done to annoy you?' I saw Jonquil, her lips unmoving, immediately replace her receiver. Then Sam replaced his. My God, he really was going too far—ringing her up in the office...

His expression had darkened. He began to type and the keys sounded like the firing of machine-gun bullets. 'Hell hath no fury' can apply to men as well as women. Had Jonquil been right when she said I didn't take Sam's behaviour seriously enough? He was looking so angry...

Perhaps anger is infectious too, for Rawden had been typing away rather viciously for some time. I thought he was doing an article, but suddenly he ripped the paper out of the machine, turned to Sam, Kate and me and said: 'I feel better. I have written a hate letter to that Swedish bitch and I am going right out to post it.'

'Bully for you,' said Sam and Kate burst out laughing.

As Rawden charged out, like a soldier going into battle, we all laughed. It was so ridiculous. Kate gasped: 'Rawden is amazing. First he threatens suicide because his love has gone and now he's having a whale of a time hating. You've got to hand it to the Strines.'

But Rawden went even farther. The devil was in him that morning. Just before lunch he went into the 'goldfish-bowl' and spoke to Jonquil. And then—they went out to lunch together.

Sam's face would have to be seen to be believed. Kate caught my eye and a dreadful wave of laughter surged through us, as with schoolchildren who must not, must not laugh—yet the giggles bubble up like invisible vomit. Hysteria. We were all going mad in Heart-break Corner...

'Well!' gasped Sam. 'Of all the bloody nerve! Did you ever see the like!'

Kate, valiantly containing her suppressed giggles, fled to the washroom. I found that the absurd laughter had almost made me cry and lit a hasty cigarette. Thank heaven for tobacco. A lover is only a lover, I told myself, but a good cigarette is a smoke.

'She did that deliberately to upset *me,*' said Sam. 'She's never looked twice at Rawden before.'

'She has actually,' I said, 'but he's never been free before.'

'You think she fancies him?'

'I wouldn't be surprised.'

'Oh, if ever a man suffered!' said Sam, in imitation of a north-country comedian. 'I'm not myself any more and that's a fact. Still, I don't understand what she sees in Rawden.'

'He may seem a bit dumb to us but he won't to her. She's only a kid. I expect she pictures him on horseback in the big wide open spaces, whistling ''Waltzing Matilda''.'

'Him or the horse?' said Sam. 'Oh, to hell with everything. Got any more filthy letters?'

'No. You've had your ration for today.'

'Then I might as well go and jump in the river,' he said, departing quite cheerfully, and I thought I guessed why he felt better. He believed that Jonquil had accepted Rawden's invitation as a gesture of defiance to him, Sam. Thus he felt he had evoked a response from her. There was something definite to bite on. I felt slightly more cheerful myself. At least the office hadn't been dull. I went over to the pub to have a drink for lunch.

Rawden and Jonquil were there, tucked away in an alcove, but they didn't see me and I sat where they had their backs to me. I sank some vodka. It tasted good. Perhaps I'd take up lunch-hour drinking as a regular habit. Then a man came into the pub who, for a second, reminded me of *him*. Something about the shape of his nose and the way his hair grew. The reality of hopelessness came crashing back. This pain...

The afternoon brought more drama. Sam 'rang Jonquil up' again. I heard him say: 'So you'll go out with him but you won't even speak to me. Why?' Jonquil replaced her receiver as she had done before, then went over to Mrs Bellen and spoke to her. A minute later La Bellen, wearing a wide-brimmed hat today, let herself out of the 'goldfish-bowl' and came cruising directly towards our corner.

'Enter Fanlight Fanny, the Nighclub Queen,' muttered Sam. 'What does *she* want? She usually ignores us hoi-polloi over here.'

She had arrived, accompanied by wafts of perfume. She smiled dazzlingly at Sam. 'Mr—er—' she began, couldn't remember his surname, so altered her greeting to, 'Sam! You're being very naughty. We all know that Jonquil is pretty as a picture, but I really cannot allow you to telephone her in the office. She has her work to do. Forgive me for sounding so frightfully schoolma'amish, but I have the Woman's Page to run. Business and pleasure don't mix, do they now?' Another radiant smile.

'I suppose not,' Sam said meekly.

'Then you'll be good in future?' Her expression was coy. Her false eyelashes were flapping up and down like bat's wings.

Sam hadn't a chance. He might mock her behind her back, but her presence overawed him. He'd gone crimson and now put on a tortured little smile. 'Er—yes,' he said.

'Thank you! Oh, you naughty men!' She waggled a crimson-nailed forefinger at him and sailed away, her wild wide-brimmed hat waving in the breeze.

'Christ!' said Sam.

Then he put his head down on his type-writer and laughed. His shoulders shook. Snorts and gurgles came out of him. Heads turned. The sound of the laughter was almost weeping. He couldn't stop. At last he half-buried his face in a hand-kerchief and dashed out to the washroom to recover in private.

'Poor old Sam is in a bad way,' said Rawden. 'There's nothing special about that girl he's so keen on, you know. Good looks but not much else. She's a virgin too.'

'How do you know?' Kate asked.

'I asked her, of course. It's best to find out important things straight away. I never touch a virgin.'

'I shouldn't think a virgin would particularly want to touch you,' said Kate. 'I wouldn't.'

'You're no virgin.'

'I was once!' Kate was quite indignant.

'Don't squabble, children,' I said.

'No, Auntie,' said Kate and Rawden gave me a sudden, sad little grin, as if he were saying: I'm putting on the act of my life. How am I doing? Behind all the defiance and the nonsense he was the same man I'd seen on the roof, flattened against the chimney-stack, saying he had nothing to live for.

This is the great error. We should not need something to live *for*. Life should be enough. To see the green on the trees in spring. To see the sky, always there, always so beautiful. To see a river flowing by, ever-changing, never-changing. To watch the sun rise in the early morning, making a picture of such beauty that it takes your breath away—makes you pray, even if you don't know you're praying. Life itself should be enough to live for. So—why isn't it sometimes? What devil gets into us, calling itself love?

I can't believe that I'll never see you again, my darling, just because your wife is cutting up rough. When you come back from Italy—such a long time ahead —three weeks—three centuries—will you ring me? It's Hope that's the Devil. Without any hope at all, I really would settle for the emptiness and learn to live with it. If you were dead—well, I'd have to accept that, wouldn't I? I'd be free! Does that mean I'm wishing you dead? Oh, no—no—and yet—am I?

As long as you're still alive, some-where, I shall go on hoping and be no more free than I was before. Love does not let go. It's a steel trap.

Rawden lingered after office hours. 'I'm in a trap, Auntie,' he said. 'I've done everything. I've written her a hate letter and I've taken another girl, a very pretty girl, out to lunch. But I don't feel any different. Tell that to the poor devils who pour out their hearts to you on paper.' He looked at me with his sad snake-eyes and went away. Sam had left some time ago, looking grey and shrunken, another headache coming up.

Kate had gone off with Andrew for another bed-night. As they left together Andrew's face had worn that Pan look. He was outside himself. When he came back into himself, then, the reckoning. Kate had stirred the primitive in the public school trainee. When his training came bashing back where would Kate be? Probably contained within the image of the 'immoral woman', with whom a man like Andrew should have no truck. Definitely letting the side down. Not cricket and all that.

My mad thoughts, whirling. I must sign these letters and go home. Not many letters. I was grateful for that now. I was so tired.

'Not so many tonight,' said Dave.

'No, not so many.'

'Why's that then?'

'We had a lot of anonymous ones. They don't have to be replied to.'

'Why do people write anonymous?'

'It's an outlet for them.'

Dave nodded. 'If I could write proper I wouldn't mind writing to you, anonymous. Nice to say something and know that someone hears, yet no come-back.

Like talking to God really,' he added thoughtfully.

'Do you talk to God?'

'Me?' he said. 'Who's talking about me? It was theoretical.'

'Dave, you are the most theoretical person I've ever met. How's your girl-friend?'

'Taking her to the cinema again to-morrow night. Trouble is, money. I can't afford more than twice a week and she'll want a choc-ice in the interval. They cost a bomb.'

'You should take it in turns to pay,' I said primly.

'I'd sooner die,' said Dave. 'I'm not a kid, letting a woman pay for me, as if she were my Mum.'

Very dignified, he was. And why did *that* make me want to burst into tears? Because everything does. And the sooner I get home, the better.

But home seemed dark when I did arrive there. My little flat had contained a light of hope before. When I reached it, however saddened or maddened I was, it used to say: Hang on. He'll come. Just wait, and he'll come. And I'd waited and he'd come.

But now? *Nevermore.* Poe's raven knew.

He'll be in Italy already. Rome. With her. Then Florence, with her. Then Venice, with her.

Will he ring me when he comes back?

'I can't travel through three weeks of time's countryside without knowing!'

Of course you can. There is nothing else to do. You will put one foot in front of the other and you will act your part.

I don't know how long I can keep this up.

You will keep it up because you have to.

Who am I talking to?

Silence.

Then the door-bell, making me nearly jump out of my skin.

I opened the door. A woman was there.

'I've come about my husband,' she said.

For a dreadful moment I thought I'd gone quite mad and was hallucinating. Surely *he* didn't have more than one wife...

'Your husband?' I whispered. 'There are no husbands here.'

'I know that, lass,' she said brusquely. 'I know you're one of these divorced women.' She said it in the same tone that some women use for 'married man'. Awful and doomful. One was beyond the pale. A monster.

Somehow all the sins of my past life came flashing before my eyes. Who was she? Was she real?

'I'm Sam's wife,' she said.

I let her in.

CHAPTER 6

She was prettier than I had expected and she reminded me fleetingly of Jonquil, although she was much older, of course, wore almost no make-up and was stodgily dressed. Her accent was north-country, but not as strong as Sam's.

'Please sit down. What can I do for you?'

She came straight to the point: 'I want

to know what's going on at that office. Sam's a changed man lately. He's had migraine before, of course, but the worst attacks come on when he's upset about something. He's in bed now, nearly blind with pain, so I slipped out without him knowing. He often mentions you. What I want to know is—are you the one?'

'Am I the one what?' I said feebly.

'The one he fancies.'

'Sam and I are very good friends, except when we quarrel over having the window open or shut, but he certainly doesn't "fancy" me.'

'Then who? Is it that film woman, Vicky? He mentions her a lot too. And there's a photographer, Kate. I must know who's having this effect on him.'

'Why don't you ask him?'

'I've asked him and asked him, but he just says there's no one. Sam's not the sort to have a fancy woman, you know. London ways aren't our ways. Whoever this woman is, she's got to leave him alone. Now, please be straight with me. *Is* it you?'

'No, it is not, and Sam has not got a "fancy woman", as you put it. Your husband is sexually faithful to you.'

'How do you know?'

I didn't know for certain, did I? No one knows anything for certain. 'There's nothing I can tell you,' I said. 'You'll have to sort things out between you. I don't intrude in people's lives.'

'But you do that advice column.'

'Letters from strangers—its different.'

'Do you make them up?'

That's the question people always ask. They can't believe that the extraordinary letters they see in print are genuine. If they saw the ones we daren't print they'd realise that we let them down lightly and that there's never any need to invent a letter.

'No, I don't.'

'You must know a lot about life then, doing that job.'

'It doesn't follow.'

'Look, I'm desperate. Sam has got some woman on his mind, even if it's gone no farther than that, and I have no one to turn to for help. His folk and mine are up North. We're like foreigners really. I wish he'd never left Local Government and come to London and that—that vulgar magazine. It's brought out the worst in him. He never used to be dirty-minded—'

'Oh, please don't talk like this. I can't stand it.'

'Keep your hair on,' she said. 'I'm trying to help my husband, that's all. Can't you give me a clue as to what's wrong? Is he smitten with that Mrs Bellen maybe? He says she looks like a tart.'

I knew that in her guessing she would not mention Jonquil's name because Sam would never have spoken it at home. It is dangerous to speak the loved one's name. One's voice gives one away. Impossible to speak the name naturally. As if a name were a spell...an incantation...the first word of a prayer...like *Om*.

'Doesn't Sam take you into his confidence at all?' insisted his wife.

'Sometimes.'

'Then if he can tell you, why can't he tell me?'

She couldn't possibly be as stupid as she seemed...

She got up, quietly angry. 'Well,

thanks for your co-operation. I'm sorry you've been troubled.'

'*I'm* sorry, but I will not conspire behind Sam's back.'

She left without another word and I was genuinely sorry for her although I'd been so unhelpful. She must be lonely, surrounded by cool London neighbours who seemed alien to her, seeing her husband go off every day to a world she knew almost nothing about, except that she disapproved of it, and then watching him nearly go out of his mind with some mysterious emotion. Sam was a victim, but so was she. Her faint resemblance to Jonquil interested me. Was Sam consciously aware of it? Possibly not. Should I tell him that she'd called? Trying to avoid conspiracy, I was already involved in one.

After that frantic Monday the rest of the week was quieter. Sam was off sick for a few days. Rawden didn't take Jonquil out again. Kate and Andrew were totally involved with each other. Then on the Friday Sam came back and a shoal of picture post-cards arrived from Switzerland. Vicky had not forgotten us.

137

It was very sweet of her! We all showed our cards to each other. On Sam's she had written: 'Lots of splendid flowers in the mountains—and you are allowed to pick them—even the jonquils.'

'The little devil,' said Sam, not displeased.

To Rawden she had written: 'The Swiss *eat* Swedes, but find them tasteless and indigestible.'

Kate's message was: 'Free love here and idle-vice galore,' and mine was: 'Tell me, Auntie, what is love?'

To Tom, however, she had written dully: 'The weather is fine and we have had sunshine every day. I hope the rain keeps off. Having a great time.' Oh, poor little soul!

Tom looked thoughtfully at his postcard and said: 'It's given me an idea. When's Vick coming back? Next week or the week after?' And what a good thing Vicky couldn't hear him say that, his personal indifference to her being such that he didn't already know the length of her holiday.

'The week after,' we told him.

'Why?' said Kate.

138

We had tensed up, as if Tom were some sort of enemy who might hurt one of our number.

'The Old Man's planning a feature on Canada. Between you and me, I think there's a tie-up with the advertising boys. However, he wants some "human interest", Canadians who've come over here and made good in various ways. I don't see why we shouldn't use Vick. Someone could write a piece on "Our Girl from Canada" and I could take some pictures of her. In the open air. We could nip along to Hyde Park one sunny afternoon. The week after next—it'll be June by then—we should get some sun. I'll suggest it to the Old Man.' Then he asked me: 'Vick wouldn't mind, would she?'

'I'm sure she wouldn't,' I said, poker-faced.

Tom loped off and Kate whispered to me: 'He's a bit dumb, isn't he? Fancy not knowing that Vicky is mad about him. Auntie, think how pleased she'll be. Shall we write and tell her?'

'No,' said Sam. 'Don't do that in case it falls through. Hargon may not want to use someone on the staff.'

'Oh, I hope it doesn't fall through. We'll all keep our fingers crossed,' said Kate.

'I don't see why you're so eager to throw her into the fire,' said Rawden. 'She'd be better keeping her distance from Tom, on the grounds that what you've never had you can't miss.'

'An afternoon in the park is hardly throwing her into the fire,' Kate protested and Sam said: 'She's in the fire already anyway.'

The fire. We were all in the fire. All burning like self-generated fire. 'We five are like compost heaps,' I said.

'Auntie,' said Kate, 'your filthy letters are having an effect on you!'

'Nothing filthy about compost,' said Rawden. 'Wonderful stuff.'

'That's right,' said Sam, 'and nothing like dung for roses.'

'Dung!' repeated Kate, pronouncing it the way Sam did and adding a ringing tone. 'In Chinese that means "to understand". *Wo dung* is "I understand".'

'It sounds to me,' said Sam, 'more like someone trying to stop his dire-rear.

How come you know Chinese?'

'I don't,' laughed Kate. 'Andrew and I went to a Chinese restaurant last night and the waiter taught us that much.' Then she went off to the dark room to develop some prints, Rawden went out on a story and Sam turned to me eagerly: 'I've been waiting to have a private word with you. What's been happening while I was away?'

'Nothing special.' Did he know his wife had come to see me?

'Has Rawden been taking her out?'

'Not to my knowledge. He doesn't bother with virgins.'

Sam smiled a little. 'Yes, I knew she was a good girl. I wish she wasn't and yet I'm glad she is.'

'You're not going to start pestering her, are you? You're fit again now, Sam. Stay that way. Forget what happened and she will too.'

'Forget? I've thought of nothing but her all the tme. I've bought her some stockings. Very fine, expensive ones. Beautiful. She can't fail to like them. Wait, I'll show you.'

Intense and eager as a child, he showed

141

me the pretty, fragile stockings in their transparent envelope. 'Can't you just see them on her legs?' he said.

'She may not accept them. Don't risk it.'

'I'm not going to risk a scene at the office, if that's what you're afraid of,' he said. 'I don't want old Fanlight Fanny bearing down on me again. No, I've found out her address from the telephonist. I'm going to post them to her to-day, with a little note—nothing sloppy— just apologising for any embarrassment I caused her and asking her to accept my gift to make up for it. Surely no one could object to that! She might even wear them on Monday! If she does it'll be a sign and I'll ask her out to lunch.'

What do you do with a man who is living in cloud-cuckoo-land? I was left speechless. I simply couldn't squash him, even though I knew he was asking for trouble. He looked so hopeful! Oh, God, let him enjoy his little bright hope while it lasts...

I was thankful he hadn't mentioned his wife, so I didn't either.

The weekend passed ploddingly and

Monday came. Sam was calm, white-faced and wearing his best suit. He arrived early and sat watching the 'gold-fish-bowl'. Jonquil swam into view, wearing a trouser-suit.

Sam looked at me and said, *sotto voce,* 'Maybe she's got them on under those pants.'

'How do you intend finding out?'

'I could go down on hands and knees and peer up,' he said, with a wild giggle which shattered his artificial calm. He went to the washroom. Jonquil must have been watching him, although she hadn't seemed to be so doing, for suddenly she came striding across the office, placed a flat parcel on his vacated desk and hurried back to her own department. Sam returned and saw the parcel. 'What's that?'

'Your girlfriend put it there,' said Rawden. 'Maybe she bought you a present, Sam. She's succumbed to your primitive charm after all.'

Sam was staring at the parcel, recognising the size and shape.

'Aren't you going to open it?' Rawden was curious.

'Not with you breathing down my neck,' said Sam. 'Bugger off, there's a good lad.' Rawden raised his eyebrows but obeyed. Sam waited until Rawden was busy typing then quickly unwrapped the parcel. It contained the stockings and a note. He read the note and passed it to me. I read: 'Dear Sam, Thank you for your letter and your apology. I cannot, however, accept these stockings from you, so I am returning them. Please leave me alone now. Jonquil.' I handed the note back, just shaking my head in sympathy.

He tossed the stockings across so that they landed on my desk. 'You have them. They shouldn't be wasted.'

'Why don't you give them to your wife?'

'She wouldn't wear fine ones like that.'

'Nonsense! She'd love them!'

'She'd think I'd gone barmy, buying something so expensive and useless.'

'Haven't you ever bought her anything frivolous?'

'Don't be daft,' he said.

Kate, who had been eavesdropping

like mad and guessing what had happened, wheeled round and said: 'Auntie's right. You should give your wife frivolous things sometimes, as if she were what you'd call a "fancy woman".'

'You all know too much about my business,' said Sam.

'And whose fault is that?' flared Kate. 'You don't exactly hide your love-life under a bushel.'

'A rose on a dung-heap, that's Sam's love-life,' broke in Rawden.

'Oh, you're a diabolical lot,' said Sam. 'Sometimes I wish I'd never left Local Government.'

Meantime I was looking at the stockings. 'They're not my size,' I said. 'How did you find out Jonquil's size?'

'I got her the same size as my wife takes.'

'Then give them to your wife!' Kate and I said together.

'You two are like the bloody Mothers' Union!' protested Sam.

'That's right, Sam, don't give in to them,' said Rawden. 'If I were you I'd take them back to the shop and get your money back; or exchange them for something else.'

'I'm not going back to that lingerie shop,' said Sam, with a shudder. 'I've never felt such a fool in my life. The assistant was a bit like Fanlight Fanny. If Jonquil knew the ordeal I went through for her sake—' He was laughing, in that awful, close-to-tears way and suddenly Hargon's secretary appeared among us:

'He wants you, Sam. Now.'

'I'm glad someone does,' said Sam, then, collecting himself, 'I wonder what I've done.'

We watched him vanish into the editor's kingdom of frosted glass.

'Perhaps the Old Man's going to tear a strip off him for perverting the morals of young girls on the staff,' suggested Rawden.

'Do you think Fanny might have reported him?' asked Kate.

'Surely not,' I said. 'He hasn't done anything!'

'That could nark Fanny,' said Rawden. 'She asks for it all the time.'

'Oh, don't be so crude,' said Kate.

'Sorry, Ma'am.'

Sam returned, looking distressed.

'Seems I've made a mistake,' he said. We waited, with baited breath. 'I got an Answer wrong. The Question was: "Who is Pygmalion?" and I gave an account of the Pygmalion and Galatea legend, then added something about Shaw's play, but I said that the Professor and Eliza got wed in the end—but in the play they don't. Only in the film and the musical. There's a whole pile of letters of complaint from readers and the Old Man says I've got to write and apologise to each one of them. He was really shirty. It's a bit thick, seeing it's the first mistake I've ever made in my column.'

'What lousy luck,' I said. 'Never mind, I'll lend you my secretary. If you dictate a stock letter and give her the names and addresses she'll do it for you.'

'Will she have time?'

'This week, yes. I'm still in the midst of the porn wave, so a lot of the stuff is anonymous. No S.A.E.'s. Bear up, mate.'

Sam busied himself in composing the stock letter of apology for his heinous error and at least it took his mind off stockings and Jonquil. I was glad to see that, in a sense, his job came first. He was genuinely concerned over the editor's displeasure. On a newspaper or magazine you can get fired for incompetence and that would hardly happen in Local Government. Sam had given up a secure job for an insecure one. If he started making mistakes he was risking his livelihood; and he'd made this one because he'd been in emotional turmoil and not checking his facts meticulously. He'd wasted too much time pretending to look things up in the library and not really doing so.

When his draft letter was ready we took it to my secretary and explained the situation. She was a sweet girl and made no objection at all, nothing on the lines of 'That's not my job.'

'I'll do them a few at a time, in between Auntie's letters,' she said, 'then all you'll have to do is sign them.'

'I'm very grateful,' said Sam, adding, in a moment of inspiration: 'What size stockings do you take?' She told him. 'Same as my wife takes,' he said. 'I'll give you a pair of stockings as a grand reward.' She protested but he'd have none of it and as we walked away from her he said: 'That's what's known as "a good deed in a naughty world".'

'Hers or yours?'

'I was thinking of mine actually, although I admit I'd prefer a naughty deed in a good world. I'll take her the stockings now. I can't bear the sight of them. Why didn't you warn me?'

'I tried to.'

'Not very hard. You must have guessed what would happen. I can't think what to do next to please her.'

'Do as she asks and leave her alone!'

'I can't,' he said. It was true. His will had gone. He was compelled. 'Are you doing anything for lunch?' he asked me.

I didn't want a lunch-hour with Sam. I'd had enough of him this morning. But that sad look in his eyes was too much for me. I was about to say 'No' but he'd seen my hesitation. 'You're bored to death with me and I don't blame you. Sorry I asked.'

'Silly,' I said. 'I'd love to have lunch with you. Let's go to the boozer, then I can have my vodka-ration and you have a soft drink and a sandwich. Okay?'

'You're a good lass,' he said, making my eyes sting with those tears ever lurking just below the surface.

He took the stockings to my secretary, then we crossed the road together. For an hour we sat in the pub and Sam talked about Jonquil and his feelings for her. He insisted that it 'wasn't just sex'. He'd love to go to bed with her, of course—what man wouldn't?—but his emotions were on a higher level than that sort of thing. 'It's like I feel sometimes when I hear certain music,' was the nearest he could get to it. 'That Sixth Symphony by Tchaikowsky. The Pathetic. When I was ill I listened to it on the radio. My wife was out shopping. I cried my bloody eyes out. I think Tchaikowsky must have gone through something like what I'm going through. The anguish!'

The outpouring went on and on and there was no need for me to say a word. My function was to listen. He concluded at last: 'Do you understand any of this?'

'I've felt as you feel,' I said, 'if you call that understanding, but why one has these feelings for one particular person I don't know. There's a religious element

150

in it.'

'But I'm not at all religious,' said Sam. 'I'm C. of E. on paper because my parents had me christened, but I never go to church.'

'You pray though, even if you don't know what you're praying to.'

'How do you know that? It's true. I've been praying during the past week or so —for the first time since I was a kid.' He paused, then said: 'You mentioned that you've felt as I feel.' He looked at me en-quiringly.

'It's time we were getting back,' I said.

'Lord, yes, I'm in the Old Man's black books enough without taking an over-long lunch-hour. I must try to do a really interesting column this week. I've been neglecting it.'

He worked hard that afternoon, really concentrating instead of going into a daydream and staring at Jonquil through the glass. But next day he had regressed, or taken a step forward, according to how you look at it. On his way to work he had bought a nosegay made up of 'sweetheart roses', small, exquisite and deeply red, their stems bound in silver foil. There was a pin attached and the posy was meant for a woman to wear. He took this and laid it on Jonquil's desk before she came in. As it was early only a few people saw him, but he didn't care about making a fool of himself. He was beyond it. He looked excited and almost happy when he came back to his own desk. I found myself hoping very much that Jonquil would soften and pin the charming little bunch of roses to her dress. It seems so cruel to discard a gift of love. Would she discard it? Or would she be kind?

CHAPTER 7

Jonquil did not exactly discard the offering, in that she didn't fling it into the waste-paper-basket; but nor was she kind. When Mrs Bellen came in, wearing a tight-fitting black suit and a red hat with black velvet roses figured on the brim, Jonquil offered her the 'sweetheart roses' and pinned them on to the older woman's lapel. La Bellen made dramatic gestures of gratitude. The colour of the flowers happened to be right for her outfit. And Sam watched this pantomime without a vestige of expression. The hurt went too deep to be shown. None of us teased him that morning and when he opened the window wide I didn't say a word, even though rain was blowing in.

We all worked solidly. It may have seemed, from the way I'm talking about our office life in Heartbreak Corner, that we did no work at all. In fact we spent most of the time working. It's just that the inbetween bits, the real-inner-life bits have stuck in my memory. It's rather like remembering the War. You tend to forget the minute-by-minute drudgery that went on for years on end and remember only the bright moments and the black ones. So much of time is just plain ordinary.

I was noticing, however, that a whole week without *him* in the same country as myself was beginning to make me see my telephone as ordinary. When it rang I knew for certain that it wouldn't be *him*, so I lost my panic-feeling about it. It lost its black magic. It was a machine and nothing more. The only reason I had a telephone at home was in case *he* rang. There is no point in having a telephone at home unless you are in love and have hope. So why didn't I get rid of my home-telephone and save the money? If it rang now it would be only an interruption of solitude, someone wanting something. But I knew I wouldn't get rid of it yet. He just might ring me, after Italy. Suppose he died. Would I get rid of my home-phone then? Yes.

How about if he murdered his wife? Would you still love him?

'I'm not sure, but I think probably, yes. I'd hide him under the bed, protect him from the police, be the real little Bette Davis.

You wouldn't, you know.

Wouldn't I?

Who am I talking to?

Tap-tap-tap of the typewriter. I was getting my column ready. A variety of readers' letters and my replies. This was the 'real' job. The S.A.E. stuff was only by the way. Hargon suddenly appeared by my side, like the Angel Gabriel complete with flaming sword. What had I done now? But he was grinning all over his cynical face. 'Look at this,' he said.

He shoved a page-proof in front of me. It was a page for the current issue, about to go to press. At the top was my column. On the lower half of the page was an advertisement. The headline of my column was: GIRLS DON'T WANT THE HEFTY, HUNKY HE-MEN. THEY PREFER THE PALE AND PASSIONATE POETS. The advertisement said: MAN—BE BIG. And there were pictures of muscle-men attracting every girl within sight and if you bought the company's product you too could be a muscle-man and get the birds.

It was delightful. A complete contradiction all in one page.

'Oh, that's fine,' I said. 'The readers will love it.'

I thought the Old Man had brought it to me to 'share a laugh'.

Not so. 'We can't let it go through,' he said.

'Why on earth not?'

'We'd lose the advertiser—making fun of them.'

'They wouldn't lose any customers by its being funny, Mr Hargon.'

'I agree with you, but *they* wouldn't. Sorry, but I want a new column from you. We can use this one next week, when we've got a different advert. underneath. What are you doing now?'

'Getting the next one ready.'

'Can I have it by four o'clock? In fact I *must* have it by four o'clock. Sorry, but there it is.'

The Lord and Master marched back to his frosted glass kingdom, or prison. The advertisers were his gaolers. And I had to put my skates on with a vengeance. The work was done by four. I took it to him. 'Good girl,' he said.

That is how a nice little joke gets squashed underfoot. The readers *would* have enjoyed it. Oh, to hell! Who'd be a journalist? However, the small emergency had at least stopped me from brooding about my bruised soul, which was a good thing. Except that I now got the backlash. I felt empty and exhausted. I signed my little pile of letters mechanically. Dave collected them. Sam had gone home, in his quiet misery. So had

Rawden. Kate was still around. 'Andrew's seeing the Old Man about the cottage,' she said.

'Oh, yes, you want it for next week, don't you?' I knew nothing about this mysterious cottage. 'Is Andrew a personal friend of Hargon's?' I asked.

'There's a connection. Hargon's brother went to the same school as Andrew. Old Boy network. I don't approve of that sort of thing,' she added, rather defiantly, 'but a cottage is a cottage.'

'What does the Old Man use it for then?'

'Auntie—you to ask that?'

'Oh, pardon me for living.'

She whispered: 'They say he took La Bellen there. He's an awful old ram. He never discards a mistress—he just adds. Has he ever made a pass at you?'

'Never.'

'I'll bet you're the only one.'

'Thanks for the compliment.'

She giggled. 'I didn't mean it nastily but nicely. You're enviably touch-me-not.'

How little we know how others see us...

Andrew came forth, triumphant. He gave Kate the thumbs-up sign. Arm-in-arm, they went off to the pub. I bought a half-bottle of vodka from the off-licence and went home. I know I am drinking too much but I don't care. I need the anaesthetic. My heart has been amputated, you see. I can't stand the pain without dope. A heart cannot be amputated. It doesn't stick out, like a limb. Mine did. It stuck out a mile. Now it's been chopped off.

Who am I talking to? Darling—come back!

Wandering drunkenly round an empty flat. Calling out to hopelessness. A certain awful joy in the misery. Self-dramatisation. I really am like a character in those films I used to see! And no more real than they were. *Tell me, Auntie, what is love?* I grabbed a book from my shelf and opened it. And here was co-incidence with knobs on. I read: 'In my medical experience as well as in my own life, I have again and again been faced with the mystery of love, and have never been able to explain what it is...Love "bears all things" and "endures all things''. These words say all there is to be said; nothing can be added to them. For we are in the deepest sense the victims and the instruments of cosmogonic "love"...Love is man's light and his darkness, whose end he cannot see... Man can try to name love, showering upon it all the names at his command, and still he will involve himself in endless self-deceptions. If he possesses a grain of wisdom he will lay down his arms and name the unknown, *ignotum per ignotius* —that is, by the name of God.'

Thus C.G. Jung, in one of my favourite books, *Memories, Dreams and Reflections*. Am I ready to 'lay down my arms' and give all this love that's burning inside me to 'the unknown'? I'd like to, but I can't. I still need a man. My body tells me so. How drunk I am. I mustn't do this again. Good grief, I've nearly emptied this bottle. Is that the door-bell ringing? It can't be. I must be hallucinating.

But I was not. It rang again. Suppose it was *him!* Suppose he came in and took me in his arms and said: 'I've left my wife and come to you because I love you

159

and nothing else matters.' And then surely there would be a burst of Rachmaninoff and our closely embracing figures would be seen in outline against a sky crimson with the dawn...

Again the bell rang. I just *might* be—darling?

I opened the door. A man stood there all right. Rawden. And from the look of him he was as sloshed as I was. His snake-eyes had a hot glow.

'What do you want?' I said.

He answered: 'You.'

Can any among us look back on his life and say honestly that he has never had such a moment of madness and known that it was wrong in every way and gone on with it just the same? What is love? It certainly wasn't that. That was two drunken animals getting together. There was an element of nightmare compulsion about it. When morning came and we found ourselves still naked in each other's arms we could hardly look at each other. We were shy and embarrassed.

'Gosh, Auntie,' muttered Rawden, 'what must you think of me?'

'We were drunk. These things happen.' I felt sick with infidelity. What sort of a lover was I, throwing myself into the arms of an unhappy and intoxicated youth, years younger than myself, only a few days after *he* had left me?

'What sort of a man am I,' said Rawden, 'feeling about Ingrid as I do, and then after only a few days—'

'I know. My God, look at the time. We'll be late!'

The practical business of getting ready for the office and pouring black coffee into ourselves to disperse the fuzziness of our brains brought back a kind of normality.

'I'll go first,' he said. 'We'd better not arrive together. You won't tell the others, will you?'

'Of course I won't. And don't you either!'

Then we managed to laugh a little.

'We're a couple of old bastards,' said Rawden.

'Forget it. If anything good comes out of it it'll be that we'll neither of us hit the bottle so hard in future.'

'You're right there, Auntie. Whew!'

He didn't seem to notice the comedy of the fact that he still called me 'Auntie'. Oh, think of it as funny. 'Laugh, Clown, laugh,' as Vicky would have said.

I lingered with a cigarette after Rawden had gone. Tonight, when I came home, I wouldn't bring any drink with me. I'd read Jung instead. I'd try to get *back*...to where?...to the blankness?... blankness is dangerous...look what happened last night...no, stop looking at it. Either laugh at it or forget. And especially, *Auntie,* stop taking yourself so damned seriously. It's all the same a hundred years hence and we all just die in the end.

Then a terrifying thought hit me like a bomb: suppose I got pregnant by Rawden! This was just too ghastly to contemplate, but I went on contemplating it in the Underground and, blow me, when I started work that morning one of the first letters I read said: 'I am in trouble. I slept with a man only once when we were both rather drunk and now I am going to have his child.' This was quite a routine sort of letter—I received many such—but fellow-feeling made me take extra trouble over my answer, instead of relying on my 'stock letter' for such cases.

Rawden and I studiously ignored each other all morning. Andrew caused welcome distraction by bringing his sword to the office. He described the looks he'd received when carrying it in the Underground. Why had he brought it? To take it to a special place to be cleaned, in the lunch-hour, and then he and Kate were going to take it with them to the cottage.

'We shall, of course, place it between us in bed,' said Kate, 'like the weirdies of olden days.'

It was a splendid sword. Everyone admired it and Andrew was full of pride and delight. He 'knighted' Sam, with due ceremony, and Sam said: 'From now on, I shall be known as Sam the Posh. I shall talk about "barths" and "parths" instead of "baths" and "paths".'

'No, don't, Sam,' said Kate. 'We love you as you are,' and Sam: 'I wish everyone did.'

But Jonquil was out at a fashion show that day, so he was temporarily free of her presence. We all just worked. At the end of the week Andrew and Kate departed for their 'love-nest', complete with clean and shining sword, and on the following Monday, Vicky came back. She was tanned and laughing and full of stories about her holiday. And she was so eager to see Tom again and trying not to show it. Then she had a happy moment.

Tom came over to her desk. 'I've been waiting for you to come back,' he said.

'Have you, Tom?' Suddenly very shy, and incredulous too.

'Yes. We're doing a feature on Canada.' He pulled up a chair, sat down next to her and began to explain. The glow which Vicky gave out was almost visible and when Tom had gone again she leaned back in her chair in a state of bliss. Then she came over to my corner, sat down in Kate's empty chair, swivelled it round so she was facing me and said: 'This afternoon, in the sunshine, he is taking me to Hyde Park to be photographed. Did you know?'

'I knew the plan. I wasn't sure that the Old Man had okayed it.'

'He has. I take back all the nasty

things I have ever said about the Old Man. He is an angel in disguise. I love him. I love everyone. Auntie, I can't believe it! On my first day back! Oh, God, You up There,' and shook her fist at the window, 'don't You dare let the sun go away! You keep it shining! You hear?'

Apparently He did, for the sun went on shining all day and Tom, complete with camera, set off with Vicky to Hyde Park.

Such a small beginning. But that was how it began.

CHAPTER 8

'Know something?' Sam said to me next morning. 'I think Vicky and Tom have had it off together. Quick work, eh?'

'Don't be such an old gossip.'

'I'm not blaming them, lass. I'm envious actually. An afternoon in the park with her is my idea of bliss.'

'With Vicky?'

'No, no—*her*. She's still treating me like a bad smell. You saw what she did with my roses?'

'Yes, and I thought it was cruel of her, but you are becoming rather a glutton for punishment. You invite rebuffs.'

'I suppose they're better than nothing at all,' he said. 'At least she knows I'm here. Do you know anything about scent? What's that stuff you used to wear sometimes?'

That 'stuff' had been expensive, exotic and erotic and I had worn it on the days when I was going to meet *him*. I would probably never wear it again. 'Why do you want to know?' I asked.

'If you tell me what it's called I'll buy her a bottle.'

'Sam, you simply mustn't!'

'I don't see why not. I want to give her something beautiful and that scent is. Be a good lass and tell me what it's called.'

Weak-minded as I am, I told him. He blanched slightly when I also told him the price. 'I could get a miniature bottle,' he said.

'The price I've told you *is* for the miniature bottle.'

'Christ!' said Sam. 'Eh, if ever a man suffered!' He looked across at Vicky, who was busily typing, catching up on the backlog of work caused by her holiday; then at Tom, who was leaning back rather arrogantly in his chair and kept giving Vicky sidelong glances. What *had* happened in Hyde Park?

I was soon to know. Vicky wasn't a reticent type. When Tom and Rawden had gone out on jobs and Sam had left early for lunch to go on a scent-hunt Vicky looked round at me, beamed, came across, sat in Kate's chair again and said: 'Auntie, I am truly and completely in love for the first time in my life. I knew I was already really, but yesterday proved it to the hilt. And—' She hesitated, dropped her voice: 'And he feels the same. We had the most wonderful afternoon! I still keep feeling as if I'm dreaming. It shows you that you must never give up hoping. I almost had. In Switzerland I went for long walks and told myself there was no hope and I must be like Masha in Chekhov's *The Seagull* and "tear this love out of my heart, tear it out by the roots". And now—it makes me think maybe there is a God after all—that He tests you to the uttermost, and then, when you think you're beaten—He heaves you up out of a black mud of hell and puts you on a golden cloud! It is a dream come true. I love Tom and Tom loves me.'

'Tom also has a wife and family.'

'Oh, you old wet blanket! Why do I confide in you?' Eyes full of tears suddenly. 'I know it can't last. He and I both know that circumstances are against us. I wouldn't admire him if he were the sort of man who let his family down. They are his duty. But when you have love and happiness *now* the thing is to be thankful and make the most of it. I *will* be happy!'

Outside the window the sun had clouded over.

She went back to her desk and resumed her work, typing quickly and feverishly. Too happy for happiness. Afraid already. Most people are afraid of happiness because they know how terrible they'll feel when it's gone again. Some people will never dare even let themselves be happy because of this real fear. They keep to the twilight, where there is no great brightness and no great darkness. They miss much, but stay safe. From now on I shall be one of those. But Vicky is not. Vicky is brave.

And Tom? Nice, quiet, conventional old Tom, who had never previously guessed that anyone as unusual and 'glamorous' as Vicky could be interested in him; he must have been knocked sideways by the revelation of her hero-worship. In the office she had hidden it well, displaying her vivacity to those she didn't care about, being shy and stiff with him. In the park, in the sunshine, when there were no inquisitive colleagues around, she would have let herself go and gone to his head like a drink. And he would feel so guilty—and so glad.

On the following day he had the prints of the photographs he had taken of Vicky. The Old Man would pick out a couple of the best for use in the paper. Tom gave Vicky a set for herself and she brought them over to show me. She looked so beautiful, both as she handed them to me and in the pictures themselves, that I could have wept for her. This was Vicky as she could be, a sort of

169

ideal Vicky, and such a time might never come again.

'Darling, they are *lovely,*' I said sincerely, 'and so are you!'

'Don't I get a look-see?' said Sam.

The pictures were passed across to him. He goggled. 'Eh, Vicky,' he said, 'either Tom's a genius with that camera or I've never looked at you properly.'

' "Properly", Sam, is not the word,' laughed Vicky.

'That lass should be more careful,' Sam commented, when Vicky had gone. 'Tom is a "married man".'

'You disapprove of his behaviour?'

He flushed. 'Touché.' Then he brought something from his pocket. 'That *is* the sort you said, isn't it?' He showed me the little bottle of scent.

'That's the one.'

'How am I going to give it to her?'

'I suppose it's no use my telling you not to.'

'Not the slightest. Anyway, now I've got it, what would I do with it if I didn't? Can't waste good brass. I'm going to leave it on her desk when she's out in the lunch-hour.'

'You're mad, my love.'

'Maybe, but I've never felt so alive in my life!'

Rawden came drifting in and gave me a fleeting wink. Goodness, if Sam knew about that 'drunken orgy' he'd be really shocked. I was pretty shocked myself. I was due to start the 'curse' in a day or so. Suppose I didn't! I went goosepimply at the thought. But there had been a benefit from that night with Rawden. It had pulled me up sharply, shown me the downward path, prevented me from letting myself sink farther into self-indulgent degradation. I read Jung in the evenings now instead of drinking vodka. Rawden had done that for me. And what had I done for him? Maybe revived his confidence in himself as a male. Ingrid had dealt his vanity a bitter blow.

Sam muttered: 'Old Rawden's looking better. He's getting over that Swedish bitch at last.' But he spoke too soon, for when he called across to Rawden: 'When are you taking your holiday then?' the other replied: 'Week after next, when Kate and Andrew come back. I've just booked myself a fortnight in Sweden.'

'You're not chasing Ingrid again!' said Sam.

'You don't get something you don't chase,' said Rawden and Sam: 'I'd say you were asking for trouble.' By which time Jonquil had gone out to lunch and Sam himself 'asked for trouble' by leaving the gift of perfume on her desk.

Rawden watched him with a certain awe. 'He doesn't give in, does he, Auntie?'

'People should never give in,' said Vicky. 'When you find what you want you should go after it.' She then went out to 'meet someone' and it wasn't difficult to guess that she'd be meeting Tom somewhere for lunch. He would be too careful to leave the office *with* her. Everyone 'knew' but a fiction of 'no one knowing' must be kept up.

In the afternoon we had the drama of the perfume. Jonquil went into unexpected action. Her pretty little face lost its serenity. It reddened and she glared at Sam through the glass. We four in the corner became as if petrified. We all stopped typing at once and stayed with hands absurdly poised over the typewriter keys. Jonquil, bottle of scent in hand, marched across the office and right up to Sam. Without lowering her voice she said: 'For the last time, I ask you to leave me alone. I don't want your suggestive presents. It's time you grew up and saw what a fool you're making of yourself. You're just a dirty old man!'

She dropped the bottle on his desk and walked off.

Sam picked up the bottle and threw it after her. It missed her and hit the wall and the force of his throw had been such that the glass broke. Within seconds the office smelt like a harem. Jonquil ran into the washroom for refuge. La Bellen came out of the 'goldfish-bowl' and trundled after her. Hargon came out of his office. 'What was that noise?' he demanded, then sniffed the air.

It was Vicky, bless her heart, who came to the rescue. With her sweetest smile she said: 'I'm terribly sorry, Mr Hargon, but I dropped a bottle of perfume and I'm afraid it broke.'

'Oh, is that all.' His scowl faded. 'By the way, Vicky, nice pictures of you. I want you to write me a piece about yourself, your life in Canada, why you came to England, jobs you've done. About a thousand words. Okay?'

'Sure, Mr Hargon. I'll do that thing.'

'Good.' He gave her another smile. She was looking so very attractive and the scent was probably going to his head too. If our Vicky wasn't careful she'd find herself in that cottage—and not with her beloved Tom.

'Thank you, Vicky,' Sam said when the Old Man had retreated.

Vicky turned to him: 'You are a fool,' she said, 'to carry on the way you did, but Jonquil was more than a fool—she was really bitchy and nasty. She had no right to speak to you like that. I'm going along to the washroom to tell her so.'

'Eh, no peace for the wicked,' said Sam.

'You shouldn't *be* so wicked,' sighed Rawden.

'If my wife,' said Sam, 'had been here this afternoon she wouldn't have believed her eyes. I didn't know I had it in me!'

And I realised to my astonishment that he was quite proud of his small act of violence. But the flash of pride was short-lived. Apparently Jonquil was 'very upset' and La Bellen had sent her home. So Vicky informed us, when she returned from the washroom, where many of the emotional scenes in office life occur.

Sam said: 'I wish that smell of scent would go away. I feel sick.' He retreated to the men's washroom.

'If this goes on,' said Vicky, 'we'll all be crammed together in the lavatories and there'll be no one left to do the work.'

And we laughed, we three who were left in our corner.

When Sam came back it was obvious that his migraine was starting up again. The tea came round and he took some pills. My secretary brought Sam's apology-letters over for him to sign and, having heard Jonquil's outburst and feeling sorry for Sam, she said: 'Those stockings you gave me are really super. I shall wear them for my next special date.'

'That's grand,' said Sam, trying to smile.

The pendulum had swung. Farce was

back to tragedy.

Later, when I was almost alone in the office and Dave came for my letters, he said: 'What happened to old Sam then? I've never seen anything like it. Suppose he'd hit her with that bottle and knocked her out.'

'It was only a little bottle.'

'But he threw it hard! It shot through the air like a bullet. I think he's gone round the bend. I know if my Dad behaved like that my Mum would have something to say. Mind you, that Jonquil is a good-looker. There's no denying it.'

'How's your own love-life going?'

'Not too bad, but expensive.'

'You should take it in turns to pay. I've told you that before.'

'I've got my pride!'

'Bottoms!'

He laughed. 'You look so prim, Auntie, but you're not, are you?'

'I'm not anything, Dave.'

Many a true word...

The weekend brought some relief however. I started the 'curse'. No more need to fear a miniature-Rawden on the way.

Oh, what an escape! But the three weeks have passed somehow. You're back in England now, my darling. You didn't really mean that we couldn't see each other again, did you? You'll ring me— won't you?

The telephone had changed from a machine into a black demon sitting there, silently laughing. Was I going to let myself go through all this misery of hope again? Had I *no* control over my orgies of self-pity and obsessive telephone-gazing? The weekend stretched out. Roll on Monday.

When Monday came I felt better, but Sam was down in the dumps. He exuded such misery that one could not ignore it, yet nor dared one speak to him. He was all closed up in a prison of self-induced despair. Just before lunch, however, he peeped through the grating with a prisoner's tormented eyes and said: 'Will you have lunch with me?'

'Yes, Sam,' I said.

'I'm in a right mess,' he told me as he sipped his lemonade and gnawed a rather tired sausage-roll. I took a swig of vodka and said: 'What's happened?'

177

'When I got home on Friday my wife smelt scent on me.'

'Sam, I should think the wives of all the men in the office smelt scent on them that evening! It's powerful stuff and it didn't half spray around.'

'Oh, I told her that some had been spilt in the office, but she wouldn't believe me. She said I hadn't been at the office at all but with "that woman". "Who is that woman?" I asked and she said she didn't know but was bloody well going to find out. Except that she didn't say "bloody". My wife never swears. She went on nagging me and my head was aching and I told her so, but she said she'd had enough of "that feeble excuse". So I told her.'

'Told her what?'

'That I was in love,' he said simply. 'I told her that I loved Jonquil and always would; that I'd get a divorce and marry the girl, but she obviously wouldn't have me. I told her about the presents I've given to Jonquil—'

'And how they were rejected?'

'No. I didn't let on about that. Oh, no, I did't *want* to tell my wife about my feelings—I'd rather have protected her from it all—but she would have it, so she got it. Well! She burst into tears, went to bed, told me to keep away from her, and I slept—if you can call it sleeping—in the living-room. She let me into bed again over the weekend, but not to touch her, and she's hardly spoken to me since. I tell you, the atmosphere in my home is like a deep freeze. I've lost everything!'

'You should be flattered that your wife minds so much. When I was married and my husband went off with other women —in a far more flagrant way than you've done—because you haven't really *done* anything—well, when he did I never made a scene about it because I didn't care much. My pride was hurt, but I'd stopped loving him. Your wife loves you.'

He shook his head. 'She doesn't know what love is. She's possessive, that's all, and highly "moral". You can't understand because you haven't met her.'

'Oh yes I have. She came to see me and she reminded me of an older edition of Jonquil.'

'My wife came to see you?'

'She did. It was when you had that first bad migraine. She knew you'd been upset, she was very worried about you, and she asked me to help. I told her nothing. She rather hated my guts for that. But she cares about you, Sam. It's your job now to melt the "deep freeze". Ask her to forgive you. Be kind to her. And cut that shallow little Jonquil creature out of your heart.'

'If I did that,' he said, 'I'd die. You don't understand.'

So the situation was unresolved, but maybe it had been some relief to him merely to talk. Not that I bothered over Sam that afternoon when we returned to work, because I was faced with the problem of the vicar's wife. My post had revived this Monday. The conventional porn syndrome, flagellation, rubber macks, tight corsets and whatnot, the anonymous stuff, had died out of its own accord and I was snowed under with 'serious' letters, all with S.A.E.s. I'd dictated replies to the first batch to my secretary in the morning and the poor girl was still slaving away and now I 'continued with our next', as if the whole business were a serial story. And the first letter I picked up to concentrate on and frame a reply for was the one from the vicar's wife.

She told me in great detail all the things her husband could *not* do, sex-wise, and all the techniques she had tried to make the poor chap function. It was gruesome reading. And I 'smelt a rat'. There were her name and address, clear as clear. She lived, apparently, in some little village. In its essentials I saw the letter as a porn effort, but not anon. Which was unusual.

And I suddenly thought how easy it would be for some nut in the village, who had it in for either the vicar or his wife, to write this letter, apparently from her, in the hope that she would get some lurid reply from a magazine which neither she nor her husband would touch with their moral bargepole...if indeed they'd ever heard of the magazine at all.

I didn't know what to do. After my recent error over replying too recklessly to a 'battered wife' I thought I'd rather share the responsibility of answering this one. So I went to Hargon's secretary and asked if I could see the Old Man for a minute. She liked being asked. She hated it when people went straight to the Old Man without her say-so. So she put me, as it were, 'head of the queue', small reward for my courtesy, and within fifteen minutes I was in the Presence.

'Well, what is it?' he said.

'This letter, Mr Hargon. I'm wondering if the vicar's wife wrote it at all, or if it's someone trying to make mischief. How shall I answer it?'

He read the letter, pinkened, then said: 'I can't imagine a real vicar's wife writing this. No, it's definitely dodgy. Write to her, say you've received a letter in her name and ask for ratification that it's genuine. Okay?'

'Yes. Fine. I thought I'd better ask you first.'

'Glad you did,' he said. 'What with your "battered wife" and Sam making a hash of Pygmalion, we don't want any more slip-ups. And yet,' he added in sudden desperation, 'why do we bother? I don't think any of our readers really read. They only use the paper for pin-up-goggling and wrapping up their fish-and-

182

chips.'

'But what could be more essential,' I exclaimed, 'than dick and grub!'

He shook his head. 'And I always thought you were such a lady!'

'Maybe the vicar's wife has perverted me.'

We were both laughing as I ducked out of his office. The Old Man was awful, but you couldn't help liking him. I wondered how Andrew and Kate were getting on in his cottage, the scene, apparently, of his many illicit amours. But were they real or fictional? The chap at the Top is always rumoured about. I visualised him suddenly with La Bellen. I wondered if she took her hat off in bed.

There is definitely something in telepathy, for when I returned to my desk, Sam, who had been watching the 'goldfish-bowl', said casually: 'I wonder if Fanlight Fanny, the Night Club Queen, takes her hat off in bed.'

This was so uncanny that I made no response at all.

He then said, equally strangely: 'I don't think they should have taken that sword to the cottage. Someone might get hurt.'

'Sam, what are you talking about?'

'Kate,' he said. 'I don't trust Andrew the Posh. Never have.'

'That's only because you're an inverted snob.'

'Got any filthy letters?' he asked wistfully.

'No. Go away.' But how poor old Sam would have loved the letter from the vicar's wife. He'd have laughed like a drain.

But in fact he was dreadfully depressed and his talk was bravado. I noticed that the window was closed. He usually opened it whenever I left my desk. Why hadn't he bothered? Too wretched to care. 'Would you like some air, Sam?' I opened the window.

'Mmm, not a bad idea,' he said indifferently.

And the afternoon drifted indifferently on. I finished dictating letters. My secretary said: 'I shan't finish them all tonight.'

'Don't even try to,' I said. 'There's always tomorrow.'

'It's going to be one of those weeks,'

184

she sighed. 'When the S.A.E. lot let up for a bit, they always bash harder afterwards. Funny, isn't it?'

'Very funny. My telephone looked at me. I'm not going to ring, it said, and even if I do I won't be *him*.

I know that, I told it with silent severity. I have no hope.

Who are you kidding? it responded.

And rang.

I jumped. I grabbed it. Oh, please, God—please—

'Auntie?' A little tiny voice, but recognisable.

'Is that Kate?'

'Yes. Something awful's happened.'

'What is it, love?'

'It's Andrew.' She began to cry.

'Has he left you?' I asked.

'Yes. He's dead.'

CHAPTER 9

'Dead!' I merely breathed the word, but heads turned—Sam's, Vicky's, Rawden's. And I almost seemed to 'see' Kate in the desk in front of me, turning her head to listen to what was going on in the 'family'.

'What happened, Kate?' They were all listening, rising from their desks, coming to stand round mine. We five, Kate here yet not here...

'We had a quarrel,' she said. 'I don't even know what it was all about now, or how it started, but he waved his sword at me and I wrestled with him and he got hurt. Well, that was last evening, and it wasn't really much. I bandaged him—it was only his arm that was cut—but by midnight his arm had swollen up. There's no phone at the cottage, so I left him and ran down to the village to find a doctor. I did find one and he gave Andrew some sort of injection, then

186

drove him to the nearest hospital. They took him into Intensive Care. But they were too late. He died of septicaemia during the night. Or at dawn actually. Auntie—I can't talk any more—will you tell Hargon?' She rang off. If there was no phone at the cottage she must have been in a public call-box. Oh, Kate— poor little Kate—I spared not a thought for Andrew—the dead are free and out of it—why waste worry on them? It's the living who suffer.

'I heard all that,' said Sam, white as snow.

Vicky and Rawden nodded. Kate's clearly articulated voice had defied mechanical distortion and reached them all.

'And I was only just thinking about her,' said Sam.

I said: 'She asked me to tell Hargon.'

So I made my second visit to the editor's sanctum. I didn't bother with the diplomacy of approaching his secretary first. I simply tapped on the door and went in.

'What is it now?' he asked.

I told him. He said, 'I should never

have rented them that cottage. It's got a jinx on it.' This from the hard-headed editor, whom one would not associate with superstition of any kind. He rose. 'I'd better go down there.' He rang for his chauffeur. 'Bob? We're going to the cottage—now. I'll be with you in five minutes.' He turned to me. 'You're good friends with Kate, aren't you?'

'Very.'

'Will you come with me?'

'Yes, I'd like to. She'll be nearly out of her mind.'

'Five minutes then, in the entrance hall.'

I dashed back to my desk to collect my handbag, told the others I was going to the cottage with the Old Man, just had time for a quick wash and to slip on my summer coat, and Hargon and I arrived in the entrance hall at the same moment. Bob was already waiting with the car. He was a pleasant, middle-aged man, smart in his uniform, accustomed to being ready at a moment's notice. He asked no questions, of course, but during the drive Hargon said.

'You'd better know what's going on,

Bob. I let the cottage to Andrew and Kate for their holiday. Last night, apparently, Andrew hurt himself on that ancestral sword he was so proud of and he died of blood-poisoning in the small hours of this morning.'

'Yes, sir,' said Bob, unsurprised.

'Did you know already?' I asked.

'Er—yes. The telephonists said something.'

'They do too much listening-in,' snapped Hargon.

'I don't think they meant to hear, sir. It was long distance, so they held on to be sure that the connection had been made.'

'And then held on that much longer. Don't I know! There are no secrets in any place where there's a switchboard,' Hargon grunted. He was in a black mood, small wonder, yet I thought he was decent to rush down to the cottage like this. Not every boss would have bothered. It reminded me of a time when one of the men on the staff had been taken seriously ill and Hargon himself had taken the man home in his own car, talked to the wife and offered any help he could. He saw his staff as a kind of family, wayward, lazy, careless, un-punctual, often disreputable, but if any of them was in trouble he went straight to the person's aid. That was the sort of thing that made us respect him, however rude we were about him among ourselves. We were like kids, cursing Dad but relying on him all the same.

The drive was beautiful. We came out of the London suburbs and into the countryside. The sun was golden and the leaves were green. As evening came the beauty intensified. I watched the magic landscape and relaxed, almost forgetting the purpose of the journey. I smoked a few cigarettes, so did Bob. Hargon didn't smoke but had no objection to others' doing so. The car was well supplied with ashtrays.

It was getting dark when we reached the cottage. A light shone from one of the windows. 'Wait in the car, Bob,' said Hargon. 'I'm not sure whether we're going to stay or take Kate home. We'll have to see how she feels. I'll come out and tell you later.'

'Right, sir.' Bob spent hours of his life waiting in that car, or driving around in places where there was 'no waiting'. Pretty nerve-racking that. Who'd be a chauffeur?

By the time Hargon and I had reached the door, Kate had heard us and opened it.

'Oh! How good of you to come! I didn't expect—'

'We didn't fancy the thought of you being here on your own after a shock like that,' said Hargon. 'Are you all right?'

'Yes. I feel unreal, that's all. I still can't believe it's happened. It was my fault, you see.'

'Nonsense,' said Hargon. 'You can get that idea right out of your head. It was a one in ten million chance that that killer-virus, or whatever it was, got into the blood-stream. It was a tragic accident.'

'I still *feel* as if I killed him. I saw him just before he died. He said—he said: 'I'm sorry, Katie.'

'Oh, Kate, darling—' I put my arm round her. Suddenly she wept, which was much better than staying frozen and numb.

'Let's have a drink,' said Hargon, 'then I suggest we drive you home, Kate.'

'I'd rather stay here on my own until the end of the week,' she said. 'You see, last week was the happiest I've ever known and it happened here. I want to be alone here and think about him. I'll be all right.'

'I'm not so sure,' said Hargon.

'Well, if I'm not all right,' Kate said, quite recovered from her outburst of tears, 'I can return to London under my own steam. I'm free to do as I please. That's what we quarrelled about. Over the subject of freedom. He began to behave as if he owned me, I don't know why it made me so angry. There was nothing strange about his attitude. It was as if some outside devil got into us and suddenly we were rowing—and he picked up the sword—and for a second I was frightened of him. Well, he wouldn't have hurt me—of course he wouldn't —but my fear made me try to wrest it from him—and as he didn't really resist me much his arm was cut—and—and it was as I said on the phone.'

Hargon had found the drinks and poured three strong ones. He passed Kate hers. 'Get that inside you.'

'Thank you. You know, Mr Hargon, it *is* kind of you to come—both of you—just to down tools and come—it's amazing—'

I said: 'Kate, suppose I stay here with you overnight. How would that be?'

'Excellent idea,' said Hargon.

'But I'm being such a nuisance—' Kate began.

'Rubbish!' I said. 'I'll stay and there's no need to make further plans until to-morrow.'

'Right.' Hargon was on his feet, finishing his drink. 'I'll be off then. Take care of each other, you two. I'll be in touch.' He gave Kate a little smile. 'Bear up, my dear. Everything passes.' He went out to the car and we heard it drive away.

'Oh, Auntie,' said Kate. 'I *am* glad you're here!'

We had more drinks and sat talking half the night. She talked of Andrew, of course, of the blissfully happy times, the mutual love which seemed out of this world—and then the sudden fiendish quarrel which had come upon them like a storm.

She kept saying: 'We weren't ourselves. It was as if something had got into us. It was like Strindberg!'

At last we went to bed, she, lonely, to the bed she'd shared with Andrew and I to the small guest-room. She lent me a nightdress. She was so sweet and I felt hopelessly inadequate. But then there's nothing anyone can really do for a bereaved person. He or she has to face the dark alone.

Next morning, at about nine, Bob turned up with the car.

'Mr Hargon and I stayed at the local pub overnight,' he said, 'then he caught an early train to town and he asked me to come here and put myself and the car at your disposal.'

'Let's both go back,' I said to Kate. 'I'll see you to your bed-sitter then go on to work myself.'

'No,' she said. 'I've quite made up my mind. I'm going to stay here alone till the end of the week, in fact for as long as we rented it for. You go back, Auntie. It was lovely having you here last night, but I want to be on my own and think. Please understand.'

Bob and I exchanged doubtful glances. 'I'm not sure that it would be good for you, dear,' he said to Kate. 'Full of reminders like.'

'It's the reminders I want,' she said. 'They're all I've got. Auntie, I'll write to you. You'll receive a letter from me before the end of the week, then you'll know I'm okay.'

'All right,' I agreed. 'Write to my home address and promise me that if you feel bad and need a voice to speak to you'll nip down to that call-box and ring me, at home or at the office.'

'Bless you,' she said. 'Goodbye.'

We embraced impulsively, then I got into the car, Bob took the wheel and we were off. I looked back and saw Kate standing at the gate of the cottage, her hair blazing like fire and her face chalk-pale. She looked—doomed.

'Oh, Bob, am I doing the right thing?' I was sitting in the front, next to him.

'You couldn't have done anything else,' he said. 'I was like that after my wife died. I didn't want anyone around.' After a pause, he added, 'I expect Mr Hargon will sell that cottage now. Too

195

many bad things have happened there.'

'What sort of bad things?'

'Quarrels, accidents, people getting hurt. It's such a pretty, innocent little place to look at, but there's something deceiving about it.'

'The Old Man said something about a jinx.'

'That's a journalistic way of putting it, but it's true enough. He hasn't used the place himself for twelve months, although he had it looked after.' I was tempted to ask more, but didn't. Bob was loyal to his boss and if he allowed himself to gossip about him to me he'd feel guilty afterwards.

By midday I was back at work. I saw Hargon for a few minutes to tell him that Kate was determined to finish her holiday week at the cottage and he shook his head but made no comment. He had contacted the hospital where Andrew died, had taken charge of the young journalist's affairs and was in touch with the brother. Andrew's only close relative. Kate had no official connection with Andrew. She had merely loved him with all her passionate heart.

Hargon said: 'Don't be too sorry for Kate. If he'd married her he'd probably have made her very unhappy. As it is, she had the best of him.'

Not that this gave me much consolation when I thought of her alone in that 'haunted' place. I'd feel easier, I thought, when I received the letter she'd promised to write; and easier still next Monday, when she was back at work and 'safely' in our corner. We would look after her.

Andrew's death had shocked the office. A quietness hung over us all. There was plenty of typing but not much talking. A death shakes egotistical people back into some sort of balance, albeit temporarily. It's so important compared with other things. Wednesday passed, then Thursday. Kate's letter didn't come. I reminded myself that the post is slow and even if she'd posted a letter as early as Wednesday, I wouldn't receive it till Friday or Saturday. I tried not to worry. She had *wanted* to be alone. Her wishes must be respected.

On Friday I received a letter I could have done without. My heart sank as I read it. It was from the vicar's wife. She said that most certainly her previous letter had been genuine and she could not understand why I had doubted its authenticity. If I was so prim and strait-laced that I couldn't take a little plain speaking I ought not to be running a column which invited people to confide their problems. I showed it to Hargon. He laughed. 'We do get 'em?' he said. 'Write her a real humdinger, full of "plain speaking", and send her one of your booklets so she can "read all about it".' Then, serious again: 'Heard from Kate?'

'Not yet. She promised to write, so I should receive her letter at home tonight or tomorrow.'

'I'll go down there tomorrow anyway,' he said. 'If she's still there I can drive her back and I want to collect a few items of personal property and then put the bloody place up for sale.'

'Why? What *is* wrong with it?' I couldn't resist asking.

'Search me, my dear. All I know is that whenever I stayed there with a friend we'd end up having a blazing row and even coming to blows.'

'That could be because you have hot-tempered friends.'

'You mean that I and my companion made the jinx, not the jinx made us? Mmm. You could be right. Perhaps we made the atmosphere—which intensified—stayed in the place—and was waiting there when Andrew and Kate arrived.' I left him quietly brooding, like a Rodin statue.

A little later I found myself standing beside La Bellen in front of the wash-room mirror. 'Isn't it just too frightful about Andrew?' she said, adding mysteriously: 'You know, *I* nearly got murdered there once.' She rolled her eyes skywards as if she'd half enjoyed the experience.

'Who by?' I enquired, with more curiosity than good grammar.

She trilled a laughter-trill. 'That would be telling, would it not?'

'Well, no one was murdered this time,' I said. 'It was an accident.'

'I heard that she cut him with the sword, when they were fighting.'

'She didn't execute him, Mrs Bellen. He had a little cut and it got poisoned!'

'Why so excited?' said La Bellen and swept out. Bitch! She disliked Kate because the girl was attractive and young, compared with her.

Jonquil came in to paint her face. 'You can tell your boyfriend,' she said, 'that's he's won. I can't stand it any longer and I've given in my notice. I shall be leaving at the end of the next week.'

'By my "boyfriend", I suppose you mean Sam.'

'Of course. You've been on his side all the way and he's made my life an embarrassment and a misery. It's turned out for the best though. I've got a better job. Mrs Bellen put me in touch with someone she knew. Very helpful of her, wasn't it? She'll be delighted to see the back of me.'

'You'll be happier somewhere else, Jonquil,' I said coldly. 'I'm glad that you've found a better job. I know you're an ambitious girl.' And who was the bitch now? Bitchery is infectious, like love. As I returned to my desk I dreaded telling Sam the news, although I knew that, from a sensible point of view, Jonquil's departure was the best thing that could happen to him.

Well, I didn't have to tell him. The office grapevine had already done its stuff. He greeted me with: 'Have you heard? She's leaving.'

'Yes. She told me just now.'

He was quiet as death for the rest of the afternoon. He took a lot of pills with his tea. All this suffering...

Vicky was gloomy too, facing the blank weekend—two whole days without seeing Tom. 'I'm so free and he's so chained,' she said. 'When I think of the innocent, ordinary things we could do together—going for walks, having drinks in funny little pubs, laughing and talking together—ordinary things—and it can never be.'

'He's alive,' I reminded her.

'Oh, God yes! Poor Kate! What a selfish beast I am! I'm so lucky really! Auntie, we must take great care of Kate when she comes back on Monday.'

'You do that,' Rawden chipped in. 'Give her my love, will you? Tell her how sorry I am. I shan't be here myself.'

'Of course, you're off to Sweden, aren't you?' I said.

201

'I am, Auntie. Someone, naming no names, restored my courage on two occasions, each very different from the other.'

'Rawden, when you talk in riddles you sound even more moronic than usual,' said Vicky.

'Auntie knows what I mean,' he said. 'Goodbye, all. See you in a fortnight's time—unless I decide to stay in Sweden for good.' He left early, with the Old Man's permission, so he could catch an afternoon plane.

'He's a fool,' sighed Vicky, 'but then aren't we all? What *did* he mean by that "naming no names"?'

'I don't know,' I said, crossing my fingers.

'Auntie—is there anything *between* you and Rawden?'

Sam broke in: 'Oh, can't you girls stop chattering? My head's spinning.'

Vicky went down on all fours and crawled back to her desk, from where she peeped round at Sam like a timid little animal, then raised her hands and did an imitation of a squirrel.

And Sam laughed, in spite of himself.

202

When at last the working day ended and I was left alone in my corner, letters signed and handed over to Dave—a very smart Dave tonight, as he had a date with his expensive girlfriend—I looked with longing at the telephone. *Nevermore.* You crouch there like a raven, you sinister creature. When will you turn back into an ordinary machine again? How long does it take for this misery-making hope to die? How long?

Then I jerked myself back to important things: Kate's letter. This morning I had left home before the post arrived. The letter might be waiting. I hurried back to the flat.

And there it was, lying just inside the door, a letter addressed to me in Kate's neat handwriting. I picked it up so eagerly and opened the envelope.

'Dear Auntie—' As I read on my relief turned to horror.

CHAPTER 10

'Dear Auntie,

'I am quite calm and in my right mind as I write this. I have decided that I don't want to live any more. I fell in love with Andrew before he even noticed me, and when he did and we became lovers, I was in heaven. I had never believed that such happiness could exist. I thought it was an unattainable dream, something that you read about in novels and poetry, and sense in certain music. But for me that happiness came true. It was real and I *lived* for the first time in my life. Nothing could ever be better than what I have had, and the thought of plodding on through ordinary living is unbearable to me. I would be bitter and lonely and live on memories, and become a nuisance to myself and everyone else. I was an only child, my parents are both dead, and I have no close relatives or friends. There is no one who will be made deeply unhappy if I cease to exist. I shall not be hurting anyone. You will be upset, I know, because you are so tender-hearted, for all your sharp manner sometimes, and that is why I am explaining to you in detail. You need not be sorry for me. Now I have decided to die, I am not unhappy any more. It was the thought of facing the future that made me weep and wail. Now that I don't have to face it, I feel all right.

'There's another thing. I did kill Andrew. I didn't know, of course, that the poisoning would set in, but when I fought with him over the sword, I cut him on purpose. It gave me a fearful pleasure to see the blood flow. This, I know, was only a murderous *feeling,* nothing to do with legal murder, but it would weigh on my conscience. I killed the person I loved, killed my own chance of happiness, and now I want extinction. I haven't any romantic notions about "life after death". I don't believe that Andrew and I will be re-united in some never-never-land. I believe what Hermann Hesse is supposed to have said to a friend, not long before he died. It was:

"The act of dying is like falling into Jung's Collective Unconscious, and from there you return to form, a pure form."

'When you read this, don't leap into activity and rush down to the cottage to "save" me, for I shall be dead already. I'm going to do it as soon as I have returned from posting this, so I shall have died when the letter is still on its journey.

'Forgive me for distressing you. Thank you for all your kindness to me, especially for staying with me that night and letting me talk my head off and use you as a Wailing Wall. But most of all, don't be *sorry*. Just *understand*. I promise that I am *all right*.

'Kate.'

Of course I did the very thing she'd asked me not to do: I 'leapt into activity'. That is, I telephoned the office, hoping and praying that Hargon would still be there—he often stayed late, as he felt more at home at work than at the house where he lived with his wife. He was there now. I told him what was in the letter. I said: 'We should go down there straight away, just in case she hasn't gone through with it.'

'Yes,' he agreed, 'and I'll notify the local police from here first, so that they can go to the cottage *now.*'

Hargon, with Bob driving him as usual, picked me up at my flat twenty minutes later. We drove in desperate silence through the darkening country-side. The sky was cloudy and there was no moon. Such a black night.

But the cottage was a blaze of light and a uniformed figure was posted at the open front door.

'Police,' said Hargon. 'They're waiting for us. I told them we were coming.'

As soon as we were out of the car I ran as fast as I could towards the lighted doorway, although I knew already that it was hopeless—that Kate had not changed her mind—she had meant every word she wrote.

'You'd better not go in and look, Madam,' said the policeman, catching hold of my arm.

'I must. Please let me go!'

He did so. I went into the living-room.

She had slashed both her wrists with the sword, slashed them so deeply and fiercely with the sharp blade that she had almost cut off her hands. There was blood everywhere. Her face, shrunken and grey, was like that of an old woman. In this room there was nothing left of Kate at all.

Darkness came down. I felt an arm round my shoulders suddenly, then sank, as if into a black pit.

When I came to I found that I'd been carried back to the car and Bob was with me. 'You're all right now, dear. You fainted, that's all,' he was saying. 'And no wonder! No, don't move. Mr Hargon's with the police. He's seeing to everything.'

'I shouldn't have left her, Bob! Even though she asked me to, I shouldn't have left her—I shouldn't—'

'Never waste time on regrets. You did what seemed right at the time. We both did. She wouldn't want you to blame yourself.'

'I know *she* wouldn't, but *I* do! She was only a child compared with me! She'd have got over it. Young people think they'll never get over their heart-breaks, but they do—they do—Oh, poor little Kate!'

'She did what she wanted to do,' Bob said firmly, 'and who are we to say that it was wrong? What do we know, any of us? Now you calm down.'

With effort I obeyed him. He lit a cigarette for me and one for himself. My head was full of mind-pictures, two particularly vivid ones: Kate as I had last seen her alive, standing at the gate, with her hair so full of life and her face white as death...and I had thought then that she looked doomed and done nothing about it; and Kate as I had just seen her, lying on the floor, an aged stranger in a sea of blood. But that second picture was *not* Kate. It was nothing.

At last Hargon came to the car. 'We can go,' he said. 'The police are going to handle everything. We're only in the way. We'll be notified about the inquest. Are you feeling better now?' he asked me.

'Yes, thank you. Bob has been wonderful.'

'Bob always is wonderful,' said Hargon. 'Now what shall we do? It's pretty late. Do you feel fit enough for the long drive back or shall we put up at the pub?'

'I'd rather drive back,' I said.

So we drove back. We hardly spoke. Except that Hargon said suddenly, after a long silence: 'What a *brave* girl she was. I'd never have the guts to do a thing like that.'

Bob said: 'I agree, and now I think that she'd made up her mind even before we left her that morning. It wasn't an impulsive act. She meant it. I can admire and almost understand.'

It was way past two in the morning when we reached my flat.

'Would you both like to come in for some coffee?' I said.

'I can think of nothing I'd like better,' said Hargon and Bob: 'Oh, yes! I'm parched.' He looked exhausted, all that driving, hour after hour, and on such a mission.

Trivial things affect one even at times when they shouldn't. Leading the two men into my flat, I felt ashamed of its surface untidiness. I hadn't been prepared for 'visitors'. On my own I tended to let things go and it was such ages since *he* had come, and so near-impossible that he would ever come again, that I simply hadn't bothered about my surroundings. I don't see my home surroundings unless I see other eyes seeing them, then I see through those 'other eyes' and go hot under the collar. Even at such a moment I had time for personal vanity...the shame of it... are other people like this? I hope not, but expect they are. Let's face it, we're a terrible old lot, we humans.

'I'm afraid it's not very tidy,' I said feebly.

'We want coffee, not tidiness,' said Bob. Bless Bob!

I parked the two men in my small living-room and went to the kitchen to make coffee. I concentrated on this job as if it were very important—as if the end of the world might come if I didn't make *good* coffee and serve it *nicely*.

I actually achieved this, despite the tremulousness of my hands, the sick sensation in my stomach and the wooly feeling in my head. We drank the coffee. Bob and I smoked cigarettes. Then Hargon said: 'You go home now, Bob. You're dead beat. I'll stay a while and get a taxi later—or earlier.' For it was morning. The night was on the way out.

Bob left and drove the car away.

Hargon said: 'You told me about Kate's letter but I haven't actually seen it. Was it very private and personal, or could you show it to me?'

The letter was folded preciously into my wallet. Was it 'very private and personal'? Would she mind his reading it? Anyone's reading it? But who 'was' she to mind? Was she anyone? Well—if she was—then it would be in some existence so remote from this one that nothing we did here would matter a damn...If there is some fantastic after-life I should think those who live it regard us lot as animals in a cage, or goldfish in a bowl. They would not blame such ignorant and inferior species for anything, only feel compassion surely. I gave Hargon the letter to read. He took quite a long time over it, then he said: 'What did she see in Andrew?'

'God,' I said.

'God? There was nothing even saintly

about that one.'

'I didn't mean that. We glimpse God through the strangest media sometimes. Some people carry light through themselves, a special light, which reaches some other people. The light that was in Andrew happened to reach Kate. I don't know what that light was. I never saw it myself. But it's always happening, isn't it? Think of the number of times we see people in love and say: "What does he see in her?" or "What does she see in him?" It's the mystery of love. You'll have felt it yourself.'

'Yes,' he said. 'But not for many years. I've discarded it since as all imagining.'

'Religious feelings are a kind of imagining.'

'The more I know the less I know,' said Hargon.

'But that's right. We know nothing. When that truth dawns on us at least we're learning.'

'For what purpose?'

'God knows!'

'We're talking as if we were drunk, yet we aren't.' Then he asked suddenly: 'Has he left you?'

'Who?'

'I don't know. Whoever it was. I can always tell when a woman is "otherwise engaged".' His eyes had something of that hot-snake look of Rawden's.

I felt suddenly afraid and trapped. What was the Old Man doing here in my flat? Why had I asked him in? Why had I let Bob go and the other stay? My whole body seemed to be beating like a heart. I felt heart-shaped. Like an ace of hearts on a playing-card. Hargon began to approach me. It was like a nightmare. Please—someone—I thought desperately —

And my telephone rang.

The shrill, demanding bell came like a rescue.

'Excuse me,' I said politely to the looming figure of Hargon. As I said it he ceased to loom. The nightmarish vision faded. He was simply himself again. The Old Man, with shadows under his eyes. Quite ordinary.

I lifted the telephone receiver and said: 'Hello.'

'Look, lass,' said a quiet, troubled,

blessedly familiar voice, 'I'm sorry to wake you at this hour, if you were asleep, but I've just had the most terrible nightmare about our Kate. Are you sure she's all right at that cottage? Because I don't think she is.'

'Who is it?' said Hargon.

I covered the receiver's mouthpiece with my hand and said: 'It's Sam. He's had a bad dream about Kate.' Then I spoke to Sam. 'Your nightmare was true. She'd dead, Sam. She killed herself with Andrew's sword. Hargon and I have been down there and we've just got back. Would you like to speak to him?'

I passed the telephone to Hargon, who pulled himself together and said in a strictly editorial voice: 'Sam? So you had a dream. You must be psychic. Yes, it is true.' He told Sam what had happened and the arrangements that were being made, then he rang off, picked up the receiver again immediately and dialled for a taxi.

It came quickly. Before he left he said briefly: 'Sorry, my dear. See you Monday.'

And when he had gone I lay down on

the floor, too tired to do anything else, and saw Kate again in my mind's eye, Kate-yet-not-Kate—that grey nothing of shrivelled flesh on the floor, swimming in blood—And in the midst of it I actually fell asleep. I didn't have any nightmares either. It was a deep, black, dreamless sleep. I woke, stiff as a board, with light shining through the window, dirty-coffee cups and cigarette stubs all around, a general atmosphere of the-morning-after-the-night-before—

And I had wakened only because someone was ringing the door-bell, again and again.

CHAPTER 11

I opened the door. Sam was there.

'Thank goodness,' he said. 'I've been ringing and ringing. I began to be afraid that *you'd*—' He stopped.

'Come in, Sam. Pardon the mess.'

He looked round. 'I felt worried about you and it seems I was right. Haven't you been to bed?'

'No. I'm afraid I fell asleep on the floor. Will you excuse me while I go and wash? I've been *dead* asleep.'

'You go and have a wash,' he said.

When I came back he had tidied the room, washed the coffee-cup and emptied the ashtrays. He had plumped up the cushions and even dusted the surfaces of the furniture.

'Sam, you are an angel! You really are!'

'Try telling my wife that.'

'I'll make us some coffee. Oh, coffee, coffee.' I was aching for it. I felt a little better after washing and changing my clothes, but still very low.

'Could you tell me all about last night?' he said, when we were sipping our coffee. 'The Old Man gave me the gist of it on the phone, but I'd like to hear it from you.' So I told him as much as I could and showed him Kate's letter.

'She had guts!' he exclaimed, when he'd read it, echoing Hargon's sentiment. 'We talk about "love" so easily, then you come across a case like this. But Kate always seemed so balanced and

217

sane.'

'She was. She thought deeply and felt deeply. I'm trying to do what she asks in her letter—not to be sorry—to understand. She didn't want people to be unhappy about her.'

'That's what makes it so hard not to be. And I thought of her as "the happy one" in our little corner.'

'She was! She wouldn't be dead now if she hadn't been.'

'Well,' said Sam, 'let's hope suicide isn't as catching as falling in love.'

'Could you take your own life?'

'I don't think so. I'm too much of a coward. Aside from that, I have a lot of curiosity about life itself. There's something in me that always wants to know what's going to happen next.'

'So you'll be all right when Jonquil leaves?'

'I shall be far from "all right". Even after this appalling event,' and he gestured towards Kate's letter, 'Jonquil is still uppermost in my mind, all the time. I am a selfish bastard.'

'Only human. We're all the same.'

'I'm hoping,' he said, 'that when she's

left she'll soften towards me. If I could meet her for lunch, say, once a week, or even once a fortnight, it wouldn't be much time for her to give up, would it? She could tell me about her new job and I'd always pay for the lunch of course. Then if ever she was in any trouble she'd know she could come to me and I'd help her.'

'You won't let go, will you?'

He shook his head. 'I know I should, but I can't.

'You mean you won't. Does your wife know that Jonquil is leaving?'

'No. We're still not speaking. When I came out this morning she didn't even ask me where I was going. She probably thinks I've gone to meet *her*. Oh, let her think what she likes.'

'Do you want your marriage to break up?'

'I wouldn't mind,' he said.

'You'd be left with nothing. There are other forms of suicide than actually killing oneself. What was your dream about Kate?'

'Fantastic and horrible. I saw her hanging on one of those old-fashioned gibbets. Those are gallows on which they hung the dead after execution, as an example to passers-by. Mind you, I know what put the idea into my head. I was intrigued over the Old Man's cottage and looked up some historical background of the village. There used to be a gibbet there in the old days. It might have been on the very site of the modern cottage—who's to know? History is fascinating stuff. Everywhere reeks of the past, crimes and deaths and love affairs. It's amazing how unaware we are for most of the time. We don't even think about it.'

'Hargon said there was a jinx on the cottage but I suggested that he'd made it. He took me seriously too.'

We laughed a little.

'He's a reprobate, or was,' said Sam, with a touch of envy. 'I shouldn't think his poor wife gets much of a deal.'

'Nor does yours,' I said.

'You've got a viper's tongue sometimes!'

'When you rang me in the small hours, after the dream, surely your wife heard on on the phone and wondered what was going on.'

'She wouldn't have heard what I said. Our phone's in the living-room. I slipped out of bed and went down there. When I came back I think she was awake, but she didn't ask me any questions. If she had I'd have told her.'

'You don't want her to speak to you any more, do you?'

'No. Now I've grown accustomed to it, it's easier than before. We ignore each other and I can think my own thoughts.'

'If I were she I'd hit you over the head with the frying-pan.'

He gave a bark of laughter. 'Maybe *you* would, but I'd never have married someone like you. You're too independent by half. Vicky's the same. You career women.'

'And Jonquil?'

'She's not a career woman. She only thinks she is because she's young and part of her hasn't wakened yet.'

'That's astute of you, Sam.'

'Just because I worship the ground she treads on doesn't mean that I've gone quite barmy.'

'You worship an archetype.'

'If that's some sort of religious building then I see your point.'

'It isn't, but never mind.'

He gave a little sigh. 'I'm so glad I came here. It's peaceful in your flat. A refuge.'

He used to say that—'Darling, it's so peaceful here. A refuge.' *Nevermore.*

'Shall we go for a walk?' I suggested. 'It's a lovely day.'

We walked to Hyde Park and wandered over the grass. It was strange being with Sam on a Saturday. We talked of Kate again and of Andrew. We discussed Vicky and Tom, Rawden and Ingrid, the Old Man and 'Fanlight Fanny'.

'We're a couple of old gossips,' I said.

We had more coffee at the cafeteria and a sandwich each. We kept the crusts and fed them to the ducks on the Serpentine. Because of the fine, warm weather, there were a lot of people about. A holiday atmosphere. The trees and the sky and the shimmering water were so beautiful. Oh, Kate, I thought, how could you discard all this? She had been a photographer too, aware of natural beauty, quick to see 'pictures'. But she had thrown away the world as 'not enough' after the fullness of love...

'I wonder where Vicky and Tom had it off,' said Sam, looking at various clusters of bushes.

'You,' I said, 'are incorrigible.'

He began to smile, then his face changed. 'Don't look now,' he said, 'but we are being followed.'

Disobeying his instruction, I did 'look now', half expecting to see his wife leap out from a laurel bush, but I saw no one I knew.

'Don't look,' Sam said irritably. 'It's better if he doesn't know that we've spotted him.'

'Who? There are so many people.'

'That thin bloke in the grey suit, with a newspaper under his arm. He looks like a private detective to me. I noticed him in the cafeteria but didn't say anything.'

'I noticed dozens of people in the cafeteria and most of them are probably walking around now, as we are.' I slewed my eyes sideways to squint at the suspect. 'He doesn't look like a private detective to me,' I said.

'Do you know what a private detective looks like then?'

'No. Do you?'

'I've never seen one before, to my knowledge.'

'Then how do you know that this man—' I giggled. 'Sam, you are a fool.'

But he was quite serious. 'I wouldn't put it past her in her present mood,' he said.

'Your wife, you mean? Arranging to have you followed?'

'That's what people do if they want a divorce.' We walked on. 'Is he still following?' Sam muttered. 'Drop something and bend down to pick it up, then have a look behind.'

'You're just being paranoic,' I grumbled, but I let my handbag slip from my fingers and bent down to retrieve it. The young man in grey was following at a distance. Could Sam be right?

'Is he still there?'

'Yes, Sam, he is.'

'I told you.' He was looking quite smug. He was enjoying it! 'Let's sit down on that bench,' he said, 'and see what he does.'

We sat down on the bench. I lit a cigarette. The young man came nearer and

224

began to stroll past, then he hesitated. Suddenly he seemed to make up his mind and walked over to us. He addressed me, not Sam. He'd gone red in the face and was shy.

'Excuse me,' he said, 'but aren't you—' and he mentioned the name under which I wrote my column. 'Forgive me if you're not, but there was a photograph of you in the paper once and I kept it.'

'I am,' I said. 'Why?'

'You sent me some very good advice when I was miserable after my girlfriend had left me. I just wanted to thank you. I always read your column. It's smashing.'

'Oh, how sweet of you.' I heard myself gushing a little. 'Have you found another girlfriend yet?'

'I have actually. She's a nurse. She's on duty at the moment but I'm meeting her this evening.'

'How lovely!' I said. 'The very best of luck to you.'

'Thanks.' He grinned and hurried away.

'Eh, did you ever!' said Sam and that half-hysterical laughter rose in me. 'Steady on, lass,' he said. 'You're still pretty shaken up, aren't you?'

'Oh, Sam, I can't get her out of my mind's eye! I wish I hadn't gone into that cottage. The policeman did try to stop me. Yet I had to see—one can't funk everything—'

'There, there,' he said and held my hand. 'What are you doing this evening?'

'Nothing.'

'If it were the old days I could have invited you home for supper, but my home isn't fit to take a starving dog into at the moment.' After a pause he said: 'You know, that young man still might have been a private detective, putting on an act to avert suspicion, because he guessed we'd spotted him.'

'No, dear, he was one of Auntie's devoted fans. Kept my picture, no less. That's more than you've ever done.'

'I've got these.' From his pocket he brought a collection of photographs of Jonquil, taken in her modelling days. They were fashion photographs—Jonquil in a fur coat, Jonquil in a glamorous evening gown, Jonquil in a trouser-suit, et cetera.

'How did you get them?' I asked.

'That first time I went out with her, before she turned against me, she told me the papers she'd worked for. I went through all the back numbers, noted down the dates when I found pictures of her, then wrote and asked for prints. They let you have them for a fee. Beautiful, aren't they?'

'Yes, they are.'

'Mind you, I'd rather have had nudes, but she never did that. She's a decent girl.'

'There's nothing decent about posing in the nude, unless it's being done for pornographic purposes.'

'That's the decadent London attitude.'

Irritated, I said, 'Come on. Let's go.'

The park was still lovely, but somehow its loveliness had faded for me. I just felt very tired and wanted to go home. My feet ached. It was hot. As if I didn't have enough of Sam all week without spending Saturday with him too. Yet he was such a kind person. He'd been very good to me.

We parted at the gates. 'See you Monday,' he said and walked away, a sad man, back to the 'deep freeze' of his

227

married life.

When Monday came the office seemed too empty. There were not only the unoccupied desks of editorial and secretarial staff on holiday, but the two very empty desks which should have been occupied today—Andrew's and Kate's. I hadn't realised what a knock the sight of Kate's desk would give me. As I sat and worked at my own, I kept thinking I saw the vague outline of her red hair and slim shoulders and looking up quickly to see if it really was there. I was 'haunted' that morning. 'Ghosts' are like that: you half see them when you're looking in a different direction, but when you direct your gaze towards them they vanish. Time and time again I looked down at my letters, 'saw' Kate, then looked up quickly to 'catch' her—and nothing.

At midday a young man came to see Hargon. He had a familiar cast of features, a drawling voice. Andrew's younger brother. He and Hargon went out to lunch together.

Vicky had heard about Kate's suicide as soon as she walked in. One of her typists told her, as she had heard it from

Hargon's secretary, so everyone knew within seconds. The place was funereal. At lunch-time Vicky suddenly burst into tears and said: 'I can't bear it!' I mopped her up and took her over to the pub. She couldn't be with Tom today as he was out on a job.

She recovered herself after a large gin and showed me the autobiographical piece she'd written for the paper. It was wittily done and I praised it. By the end of the week the whole feature would be in print, complete with photographs of Vicky. 'But it's all so trivial and stupid—after Kate,' said Vicky. 'The way we all go on as if nothing had happened.' Practicality returning, she added: 'Just the same, I'm glad I wrote my "light-hearted piece" during the weekend, before I knew about Kate. I couldn't have done it this morning. I simply couldn't. Did you see that brother of Andrew's? Wasn't he like him! I've heard that he'll be very pleased to own the ancestral sword. You'd think he'd want to throw it into the middle of a lake, like in the legend— and then a ghostly arm would rise and grab it. Oh, Auntie, what am I talking about? I talk too much. We all talk too much. And I've had the most terrible piece of news—not as terrible as Kate—and yet in a wicked way, more terrible to me. Tom told me this morning before he went out.'

'What?'

'His wife is going to have another baby! So there is no hope for me at all! Not even the tiniest glimmer on the horizon.'

'Is he pleased?'

'Yes. You know that self-satisfied look men have when they're "going to be a dad". Proves their virility and all that. Not that I needed proof,' she sighed. 'He was wonderful! By the way, I saw you and Sam in Hyde Park on Saturday. I went to take a photograph of our "special place", a private photo, just for me—and you and Sam were sitting on a bench only a few yards away. Holding hands!'

'We were consoling each other,' I said.

'I know! You mustn't mind the way I talk. It's a habit.'

And I wondered fleetingly if that was why Sam had had that watched feeling, since in fact one of the 'family' had been so close.

'I hope Sam doesn't do himself in when that little bitch Jonquil leaves,' said Vicky. 'We must keep an eye on him.'

She finished her drink. 'Oh, well, back to the morgue. Laugh, Clown, laugh!' But she couldn't.

Later Hargon sent for me, to introduce me to Andrew's brother, which was uncannily like meeting a semi-Andrew; and to say that the coroner wanted a copy of the letter Kate had sent to me.

'It won't be read out in court,' he said, 'but he must see it. Everything will be kept as quiet as possible. No publicity. It wouldn't do the paper any good. I've fixed it all up.'

'I'm very grateful, sir,' said Andrew's brother, shook hands with us and left. Hargon was looking at me. 'When are you due for a holiday?'

'Not until the third and fourth weeks in July.' I remembered how I'd changed my dates so that Kate and Andrew could be together. If I hadn't done that they might both be alive now. Everything is so terrifyingly inevitable, every action leading to the next, each event born of previous events. 'Why did you ask, Mr Hargon?'

'You look as if you could do with a break straight away.'

'Really? No, I'm fine. In fact I'm better working at the moment. I'm not in a holiday mood.'

'Mmm. I can understand that. All the same if you'd rather take your leave sooner never mind about the schedule. Just let me know. You had a rough time with Kate, trying to help her, and then things turning out as they did. I can't stop thinking about it myself. I keep *seeing* her.'

'So do I.'

'We should have done as the policeman said and not gone in to look. That attractive girl!' He shuddered.

His behaviour to me, incidentally, although it was more sympathetic than usual, was essentially businesslike, as it had always been until that weird moment in the small hours of the Saturday morning. Maybe I had only half imagined that anyway. I'd been ill enough to hallucinate. All the same I was relieved that he hadn't given me the hot-snake look again. There had been something both lustful and cruel in it.

Back at my desk I came across three letters in my post written by people who had been close to recent suicides. There was a man whose wife had taken an overdose of barbiturates, another man whose homosexual lover had gone into the garage and cut his own throat after a quarrel and a girl whose father had taken a boat right out to sea and drowned himself. Dictating replies to these, as well as to the more routine letters, drained me of about all the energy I had left. I felt as if I were living in a deadly dream.

'You look rough,' said Dave, when he came to collect my letters.

'I wish people would stop telling me so.'

'Who else told you then?'

'The Old Man.'

'He looks pretty grotty himself. This office has been cold today, even though it's warm outside.'

'Yes, Dave, it has.' He was a sensitive child underneath, affected by atmosphere.

'I miss seeing *her,* ' he said, nodding towards Kate's desk. 'It was her hair. It always caught the light, didn't it? Even on dull days, it looked like a little fire over in the corner.'

I put my elbows on the table and covered my face with my hands.

'Oh, I'm sorry,' he said. 'I'm sorry. I didn't mean to upset you. I know you and she was good mates. Can I get you anything?'

'No, love, I'm better now. Off you go.'

' 'Night, Auntie,' he said. 'See you tomorrow—and you look after yourself.'

I went to the washroom to repair my face. Jonquil was there, blast it. 'He's waiting outside again,' she said, straight away. 'It really is the limit.'

'Why don't you give the poor devil a treat and let him walk along with you to the station? It would make his day. He's feeling low about Kate. We all are in our corner. Can't you show him a bit of kindness? He won't hurt you. He won't as much as touch your hand. You could have a far worse friend than Sam.'

'He wants to be more than a friend.'

'Oh, all right. But I'm not going to play bodyguard this time. You're on your own.'

She was painting her mouth very carefully before the mirror. She did it so delicately, so artistically, with her practised fingers. I found myself watching with admiration.

'Don't glare at me,' she said.

'I wasn't. I was admiring your cosmetic skill. You're very good-looking to start with and you know just how to make the most of yourself. Do you wonder Sam is smitten? Yet you won't even give him a smile.'

'Has he asked you to try and get round me?'

'No, he has not. Good-night.'

She'd been right about Sam. He was waiting outside.

'She's still in there, isn't she?' he said.

'She is and she's waiting for you to go away.'

'How does she know I'm here?'

'Search me, mate. Maybe she peered out of the loo window.'

'I wanted to ask her what she'd like for a leaving-present. I'd like to buy her

235

something really beautiful, so she'd remember me. Now what can possibly be wrong with that?'

'Go home, Sam,' I said.

He shook his head. I left him standing there. At the end of the street, however, I glanced back. I saw Jonquil come out of the office, swift as an arrow, pretending not to see Sam. He spoke, then ran after her and caught hold of her arm.

She turned and with her hard little handbag she gave him a blow across the face. She walked on. He staggered back against the wall of the building, staring after her. Passers-by stared at him. He neither knew that nor cared.

I should have gone back, to 'rescue' him. But I didn't. I was too weary and full of pain myself, too selfish and self-absorbed. I was to regret my callousness, when it was too late for regrets.

CHAPTER 12

Next morning Sam's desk was empty.

'Not like Sam to be late,' said Vicky.

He didn't turn up at all. I went to Hargon's secretary to see if he'd telephoned. 'His wife did. Another of his migraines,' she said. 'I wish *I* could take time off every time I have a little headache.'

Later in the morning my telephone rang and a familiar voice said: 'Hello, this is Sam's wife speaking. I'd like to see you.'

'Why?'

'I can't talk over the phone. May I meet you in the lunch-hour?'

'I suppose so. How about the pub opposite the office, at one o'clock?'

'I don't go into pubs.'

'There's a coffee-bar next to the pub. Will that do?'

'Thank you,' she said. 'I'll be there.'

Now what had happened? To my

shame, I didn't really want to know. I didn't like Sam's wife. She was a 'foreigner' to me. *I don't go into pubs.* Stupid bloody woman. No wonder Sam had gone berserk over a pretty face... And if he was prostrate with migraine why was she leaving him alone and coming out to meet me? That was no way for a *wife* to carry on! I was idealistic about wives, in theory, as I'd been such a hopeless one myself.

At five minutes to one I plodded across to the coffee-bar.

She was sitting there already, sipping milky coffee. Ugh! I collected a black one for myself from the counter and joined her.

'Hello,' I said. 'Sorry if I kept you waiting.'

'That's all right. I was early.'

'Cigarette?'

'No, thank you. I don't.'

I lit mine. 'What did you want to see me about?'

'Sam,' she said. 'It's confidential. They mustn't know at the office.'

'All right.'

'I can trust you?' Her eyes were lost

and frightened.

'Yes. What's he done?'

'He tried to kill himself.'

'But that's—' I remembered his saying that he'd be 'too much of a coward' and that anyway he was too interested in life, in 'what would happen next'...

But that was before Jonquil had hit him across the face, in contempt, fear and hatred; when he had been going to ask her what she'd like as a leaving-present...

'When he came home last night,' said Sam's wife, 'he had a bruise on his face and he looked terrible. I haven't been speaking to him lately, but he seemed so ill that I broke my rule and asked him what had happened. And he cried, like a baby. He just sat there sobbing, but he wouldn't tell me anything. Then he said he had a headache coming on, so he went up to bed, with his headache-pills. I didn't think twice about that, but I went up to look at him later. The bottle was empty and he looked queer. So I guessed what he'd done. I rang 999 and got an ambulance. They were very good, the men who came. They took him to hospital and I went with him, although he was unconscious. We went to Casualty, then he was carried into a little room and he had the stomach-pump. Then he was taken to a ward to sleep it off. I stayed there all night, although there was nothing I could do. This morning they said he'd had a "good night". He'll be coming home this evening. It seems they get quite a lot of—of this sort of case hereabouts—so they treated it all as run-of-the-mill—told me not to worry and all that—and that he'll be asked to see a psychiatrist as an outpatient or something— I don't know—it was all so terrible and unreal—yet happening—and I'm in the dark all the time. I know he thinks he's in love with this girl, Jonquil, because he told me—but Sam's not the sort to fall in love—it none of it makes sense—if he'd had some ordinary "fancy woman", the sex thing, prostitutes and so on—well, I don't approve—who does?—but men are men—they carry on like that—but— but *this*—I don't know what's happened to him. And I still don't know why he had a bruise on his face when he came home—I don't know anything. Do you?

That's what I wanted to ask.'

I was torn two ways. I said nothing.

'Please!' she said. 'He's *my* husband. I've got to collect him from the hospital later and take him home. I must *know*.'

'Jonquil is leaving the office at the end of this week,' I said. 'Sam wanted to give her a leaving-present. He waited outside the office for her yesterday, to ask her what she'd like. She rushed past him, pretending not to see him, and he caught hold of her—not to frighten her—just to detain her. But she's only young. I think she was frightened. She hit him hard across the cheek with her bag and rushed on.'

'As if he were some thug or mugger?'

'Yes.'

'How do you know this?'

'I saw it happen.'

'And you didn't go over and stop it?'

'It happened too quickly for anyone to stop it.'

'But you didn't go over afterwards and see if he was hurt—or anything?' She sounded incredulous. Rightly so.

'No, I didn't.'

'Why not?'

241

'I was tired. I couldn't be bothered.'

'You!' She got up. Accidentally she knocked her coffee-cup off the table and it landed with a clatter, but she didn't seem to notice. 'You!' she repeated, looking at me with horror. 'And you write that "heart-warming" column! What a fake and charlatan *you* are!' She rushed out.

What did I do? Crept next door to the pub and ordered a double vodka. I thought: It's not fair...

I thought: She was right. What a fake and charlatan *I* am! But it was Jonquil's fault! That's it, put the blame on someone else. *I* saw him in distress and *I* 'crossed to the other side'. I swallowed my drink quickly, then went down to the river. I watched the water. 'Men may come and men may go, but I go on for ever.' Water. Peaceful yet powerful. Stormy yet serene. Ever-changing, never-changing. Filling in all the empty spaces, always keeping level. If we could all be like water...

Which hospital was he at? I hadn't asked. But I could find out. It would be the nearest one to where they lived. A telephone call…I went to a public call-box. By some miracle it had not been vandalised. I was clumsy in making the call, because I rarely used public phones. So spoiled we journalists are, with our office phones. Just lift the receiver, ask for your number, and the switchboard sees to it. Or if you want to dial direct you can. So simple. None of this fiddling about with coins and listening for 'dialling tones'. However I got through.

I gave Sam's name and asked if such a person had been brought in last night after an overdose. Yes, such a person had. How was he? 'Comfortable,' they said. Could he have visitors? Oh, yes, he was going home this evening. His wife would be calling for him. When did afternoon visiting hours begin? They had begun.

'So if I came now, to see him?'

'That would be all right, dear,' said the anonymous voice.

I walked to the hospital. I found the right ward. I went in. And Sam was there, sitting up in bed, reading an old edition of our own paper. 'Hello, Auntie,' he said. 'Now how did *you*
243

know I'd made a bloody fool of myself?'

'Why did you do it?'

'I don't know. It just came over me. I wanted OUT.'

'Oh, Sam—'

'It's done me good,' he said mildly. 'I'm so glad to be alive. That's not a bad article, you know.' He pointed to one of his own pieces in the out-of-date paper. 'If I hadn't written it myself I'd think: That chap can write.' Then, 'If you know, does everyone?'

I shook my head. 'No one. I shan't tell them at the office. Your wife has covered up for you. She told me. I met her for lunch.'

'You're not bad at being on both sides at once, are you?' Coldness in the mild voice. 'One day you'll be so bloody devious that you'll fall between two stools and never be heard of again.'

'Can I do anything for you, Sam?'

'You can leave me alone.'

'I couldn't help meeting her. She rang up and asked me to.'

'But I'll bet you told her all, showed her how humiliated I'd been.' I couldn't deny it. 'Did you tell her how I got this bruise?' I nodded, then asked: 'But how did you know that I—'

'That you saw it happen? Because I saw you, of course. You looked and walked away. Not that I blamed you for that. I'd have done the same myself if I'd seen a man behaving like a moron. I did hope, however, that my wife wouldn't know. Now that you and she have got together, I'll have to do without friends, I suppose. Not that it matters. I'm still glad to be alive. As for Jonquil, I can't think why I ever wasted my time on her.'

He returned to his reading, his face stony.

'Get better soon,' I said and left the ward with my throat full of tears and my eyes aching. I felt as if a screw in my head were being turned more and more tightly. I went back to the office and sat at my desk, hoping no one would speak to me.

Some early page-proofs came round, including my own column, which I checked wearily, cynically. What a load of rubbish it was! Who was I to dish out all this half-baked advice? I couldn't even help my own friends, let alone

245

hundreds of unmet strangers. The Canada feature was almost ready too. Vicky's article and photographs were in proof form. That at least was cheering. I saw Vicky admiring it with pardonable vanity. Tom also had a copy and he and Vicky exchanged a glance and smiled at each other, a smile of such warmth and affection, both of them recalling that afternoon in the park when the pictures had been taken. I felt isolated in my corner: no Kate, no Sam, no Rawden even. I wondered how he was faring in Sweden, if he had called on Ingrid, what sort of reception he'd had from her. Why do people fling themselves at those who do not want them? It's as if there's a need for humiliation and suffering which cannot be denied. A lust for martyrdom. I could identify with it, but that wasn't the same as understanding it. *Nevermore* said the raven crouching on my desk, pretending to be a telephone.

Suddenly Hargon was bearing down on me, the page-proof of my column in his hand. 'We're going to alter all this,' he said, 'and give you a full page in the coming issue instead of only half. We're cutting out "Questions-and-Answers". It's been going off lately and as Sam's away again he's behind with his copy, so I want another half-page-worth of letters from you. Have you anything prepared?'

'Yes. I was getting these ready for the next issue. They can be used for this one.'

'Good. I'll take them straight away. And prepare a full page each week till further notice, will you? The column's doing very well. We've had good reports from the sales side. It seems you're almost top of the pops, second only to the front page pin-up.'

'I'll be getting the Nobel Prize next.'

'Why not? Or the Order of the Pin-Up's Garter. How are you?'

'I'm fine, Mr Hargon.'

'What would we do without you?' he said, looking at the empty desks. And that, from the Old Man, was a great compliment. Any other time I'd have been pleased and proud of myself, but today the praise made me feel worse. Because I knew that I was a fake and therefore my column was a fake and the whole thing was a con-trick. Sam's wife knew. Here was I, everybody's 'Auntie', professional broken-hearts-mender, and the girl who had sat in front of me had killed herself and the man who had sat next to me had tried to do the same. Maybe people would be safer if I avoided them in future...

My secretary came over, looking guilty. 'I've a confession to make,' she said. 'I've done something really ghastly.'

'I don't believe it. Tell Auntie.'

'I got two names muddled in my short-hand-book so two people who wrote in have received replies meant for each other.'

'Then that's my fault too, for signing the letters without checking them.' Usually she was so efficient and trust-worthy that I often did that, in a way that I wouldn't have done with a novice secretary.

We sorted it out and I found that it was two stock replies which had gone to the wrong people: the 'shy young man' letter ('I am too shy to approach a girl. What shall I do?') had gone to the woman who required an 'unfaithful husband' letter ('I have found that my husband is unfaithful and feel so unhappy' and so forth). The advice to the 'shy young man' would hardly be appropriate for her and vice versa. There must have been two very puzzled people reading Auntie's replies.

'I'm so dreadfully sorry!' mourned my secretary and I burst out laughing. She said: 'Thank you for not being furious.'

'Oh, what does it matter, love? We'll just write to each of them and explain what happened.'

'You mean tell them the truth?'

'Why not? You got two names confused in your shorthand-book, I was too careless to check the finished results before signing—and we're both very sorry indeed—and we enclose what the reply should have been. I'll dictate them now.'

When it was done I said: 'Thank you for telling me. If you'd said nothing we probably wouldn't have heard from those two people, but it wouldn't have done the column any good.'

'That's what I thought,' said the girl. 'It's such a *good* column. I know people laugh at this sort of thing but you always do it so sensibly and sympathetically. My parents think you're marvellous.'

So that was two bouquets in one afternoon. Paper flowers, without scent. When your mood is black there are no real flowers.

On my way home I telephoned the hospital again, to see if Sam had left safely. Yes, he had. His wife had come for him. I hadn't phoned from the office, for fear of being overheard. No one must know that Sam had been away with anything other than one of his migraines, which had been so frequent of late. I wondered when he'd be well enough to return to work. If he took the whole week off he'd miss Jonquil's departure. That would be a benefit surely...

Some hopes. Sam turned up on the Friday, so as to be, as he called it, 'in at the death'.

He was calm, friendly, very neatly dressed and had had his hair cut, which made him look younger. He had definitely lost weight and it suited him. He seemed to have forgotten his bitterness towards me in the hospital, which was a relief. I dreaded, however, the moment when he would look at the new issue of the paper and see that his column had been cut out. I had planned to say, casually: 'It's only temporary, while you were away. They ran short of copy'— although I didn't for a fact know whether it was temporary or not. I *am* devious, as he'd accused me of being. I tend to be kind rather than honest even though such kindness is false. But when he looked through the paper he made no comment at all. I waited for him to go through it again, seeking his usual piece, but he didn't. And I realised that he hadn't even noticed. That showed me more than anything else how deep his feelings for Jonquil had been, and possibly still were, for a journalist has to be a very bad way indeed to fail to notice that his own by-line is missing.

Since he'd been away there was a large number of readers' questions waiting for him and he began to select the interesting ones, working quickly and concentrating hard, not even looking towards the 'goldfish-bowl', where Jonquil was clearing out her desk. I had to go in there to find some information and asked her: 'When are you actually going, Jonquil?'

'At one o'clock,' she said. 'Mr Hargon says I needn't come back in the afternoon.'

'Well, I'll say goodbye now and wish you luck.'

'Yes, isn't she a lucky girl!' cried Mrs Bellen. 'A fabulous job with a fabulous salary.' She was beaming with pleasure at the departure of her fair rival.

'The salary isn't much more than here,' said Jonquil placidly.

'*Someone* here is going to miss you,' said Mrs Bellen waggishly. 'Perhaps he'll throw more scent-bottles around. Such drama we have!'

'Are you going to say goodbye to him, Jonquil?' I asked.

'Good God, no!' she said. It was the first time I had ever heard her swear.

When I was back at my desk Sam asked: 'When's she going?'

'One o'clock.'

'Then will you do something for me? I'll go out at twelve-thirty, so as not to be here. Just give her this.' He handed me a specially bound book. It contained the photographs of Jonquil which he had taken the trouble to acquire. She probably had prints already, but not so pleasantly collected together and arranged. He had not written in the book, but enclosed a card saying simply: 'Wishing you all good fortune in the future. Forgive me for loving you. Goodbye. Sam.'

'She won't reject that,' he said. 'Pictures of herself, and a final farewell from me. Give it to her before she goes.'

'I will.'

Just before one I saw Jonquil ready to leave. She was alone. Mrs Bellen had already gone to lunch. I took her the book. And Sam had been right. She did not reject it. 'But it's lovely,' she said. 'I ought to thank him, I suppose.'

'You can't. He's gone out.'

'Has he?' For a second she was disappointed—surely a spurned lover should stay around for more spurning or for the surprise reward of a smile. 'Thank him for me then, will you?' she said. 'He's very forgiving, I must say.' She frowned, no doubt remembering how she'd struck him and now he'd been away sick every since, until today. She didn't know how sick…

When Sam came back after lunch he said: 'Has she gone?'

'Yes. She accepted your present and asked me to thank you. She said you were very forgiving.'

'There was nothing to forgive,' he said. 'I asked for everything I got.'

'Oh, Sam—I'm so sorry—'

'Don't be. I'm glad she's gone. Yes. I'm glad.'

He picked up the paper again and began to look blindly through it. Then less blindly. 'Where's my column?' he demanded.

'They—er—left it out—ran out of copy—'

'Oh, no, they didn't. The Old Man's got plenty of my stuff. I always keep more flowing in than is actually used. And you've got double your usual ration of space. Well, blow me! Eh,' and he shook his head, 'if ever a man suffered!'

Sam was himself again.

At six o'clock, when Dave came for my letters, he said: 'So Jonquil's gone then. Everyone seems to be leaving at once.'

'Why? Who else is going?'

'Tom. Didn't you know?'

Vicky had been out for most of the afternoon, interviewing a film actor, and was now at her desk, typing her article while the interview was fresh in her mind. When she heard the beloved's name in the air, however, she stopped typing and turned round. 'What's that about Tom?'

'He's leaving,' said Dave. 'That's all I know.'

'Who told you?'

'One of the telephonists heard something.'

'You shouldn't believe everything those eavesdroppers say.'

'Hasn't he told *you* then?' Dave asked. For everyone knew that Tom and Vicky were 'that way'.

'No, he has not and I don't believe it,' said Vicky.

'Well, here he is. You can ask him,' said Dave, departing.

Tom had come from the dark-room and now crossed to his desk. Everyone had gone except us three. It was pretty obvious that Tom and Vicky had planned to have a Friday night drink together before the 'married man' went home to his powerfully pregnant spouse.

'Tom,' said Vicky, 'Dave just said you're leaving.'

'I was going to tell you this evening,' he said.

'But you can't leave!' Her voice was a cry of pain.

Tom threw an embarrassed glance in my direction and I began to gather my things together, to get out quickly so as not to be 'in on the scene'. Vicky was beyond caring about my presence, but Tom was not.

'When are you going?'

'End of next week.'

'Where?'

'To the West Country.'

'To work on a *provincial* paper?' Scorn in her tone.

'Yes. My wife comes from there.' He glanced at me again. 'She wants to be near her own folks and bring up the kids there. London isn't very good for children.'

'She is forcing your hand because she knows about me!'

'Vicky, for God's sake!'

'Good-night, all,' I said and made a dive for the door. But I heard Vicky continue: 'I hate your wife! I hate her! I can't bear it!'

Poor old Tom! He was not going to have a jolly evening.

Restless, thinking of Kate and of Sam and of Vicky, I went to walk by the river before going home. It was beautifully warm. A lot of people were still about, many of them tourists. I heard someone speaking Italian and turned to look. I saw an Italian couple walking along with an English couple. They were laughing and chatting together, the Italians occasionally trying to speak English and the English to speak Italian. That is, the English woman was trying to speak Italian. Her husband was just smiling and looking so charming—so utterly charming—

Yes. It was *him*.

Terrified of being seen, I turned round and ran in the opposite direction—and the farther and faster I ran the closer came the love which I'd tried to drive out of myself. My efforts had been futile. Merely the sight of him had brought it all rushing back.

By the time I got to my flat I felt frantic with despair—and when the telephone rang—Oh, God—it must be him—let it please be him—I need him—I love him—I know it won't be him—but please let it be—

'Hello,' said the voice on the telephone. 'Auntie?'

'Speaking. Is that Vicky?'

'It is. May I come and see you? I'm frightened!'

CHAPTER 13

Vicky came in a taxi. Her face was a mess of recent tears. Her hands were stone cold and she was shaking.

'What on earth has happened?' I said.

'We had a terrible quarrel and he walked out on me.'

'Sit down and relax. I'll make some coffee.' My coffee supply was low, I noticed I would have to remember to buy some more tomorrow.

When I returned to Vicky she was lying back in the chair as if she had no energy left. I'd never seen her like that before. Usually she was so ebullient.

'Now tell me about this "terrible quarrel".'

'It started in the office, when you were there, then we went across to the pub to "talk things over sensibly", as Tom put it. Sensibly! How can I be "sensible" when he's my whole life and he's going away in a week's time? However I did some quick thinking and I said I'd given in my notice too and go to live near his new job, then find some work. Even if there was nothing journalistic available I could always be a typist. I thought he'd be pleased that I was prepared to make such a sacrifice—that it would prove how much I loved him—but he was horrified. Not because he cared about me sacrificing my career but because he didn't want me around.'

'Did he say that?'

'Not in so many words. You know Tom. He tried to be tactful. He said he wasn't the sort of man to have two women, that he had to choose, and naturally his wife must come first because of the children, present and future. He said she knew about us and had been wonderfully forgiving, but had made the condition that he mustn't see me any more. The only way he could do that was to change his job and then she played her trump card and said she wanted to be near her parents in the old home town and all that crap. She'd already been in touch with the said parents and they knew the editor of the local rag and they'd wangled a job for Tom straight away. Talk about nepotism! The whole thing makes me crawl. How could he be so weak? Fancy promising ''not to see someone again.'' No one has any right to make a demand like that on another human being. She must be a cow—a calving cow too—and she's doing *that* on purpose.'

'Did you say all this to Tom?'

'You bet I did. I say what I think and I mean it. I'm not sneaky and devious like his wife.'

'Have you ever met his wife?'

'No, and I don't want to! I hate her! I hate him too! Except that I still love the bastard with all my heart and I'm so miserable that I feel as if I'm going mad —and it's frightening—'

'Yes, I know. Well, go on. Any more?'

'He was so static, sitting there poker-faced when I was saying all these things. I couldn't rouse him somehow. He'd made up his stupid mind and he wouldn't even argue. So the less he interrupted the more I went on. I went crazy. I raised my voice. People looked round. But I didn't care. It was like rushing headlong to some awful doom, yet I couldn't stop myself. I was behaving in the sort of uncontrolled way that he hates women to behave—so unEnglish—like a Canadian backwoods-woman—and that was how I felt. I could have picked up a whole tree and bashed him with it! Finally I said: "You're weak and cowardly, not a man at all, and I never want to see you again," and he said: "That's how I feel too," and walked out. He left me sitting there alone, with everyone staring. It was like being on a stage with a leering, scornful audience. And suddenly I was so scared. I didn't know how I could have behaved like that. I ran out into the street, but he'd quite disappeared. So I went into a call-box and rang you. I couldn't be alone!'

She flopped back again, like a doll whose clockwork has run down. 'I don't know myself,' she murmured. 'I don't know the woman who went on like that in the pub. She was someone inside me and she got out. I must be schizophrenic. All I want now is to feel his arms round me and be made love to!' She held herself closely in her own arms and rocked back and forth. 'Oh, I love him, I love him, what shall I do?' she whispered brokenly.

I gave her a cigarette. She puffed at it gratefully.

'*You* wouldn't ever behave as I did,' she said.

'We're different temperaments.'

'I *used* to be self-controlled when he was around, didn't I? But that was before he made love to me. He shouldn't have made love to me if he was going to throw me away like a rag-doll afterwards!'

'You knew it couldn't last.'

'I knew it couldn't last for ever and
262

ever Amen. Even life doesn't do that.
But, seeing that I made no demands on
him and that I was prepared to play
second fiddle to his revolting wife, I
don't see why we shouldn't have been
happy together for years, when he had
the time.'

'Then be thankful that he's finished
the affair now. You wouldn't want to be
an "other woman" for years, sitting in
the sidelines of a man's life, having no
rights, never coming first, always having
to be free just in case he has time for you,
keeping yourself to yourself in between
for fear that other people find out and
gossip. You're too straightforward and
passionate for that sort of life, Vicky.
Tom *is* being sensible. One day you'll see
it that way yourself.'

'One day! I'm not living "one day".
I'm here *now!* We had something wonderful, Tom and I. Precious and strange
and unique. It was magic. It was godlike!
Yet he sets it aside because of convention
and a nagging wife. He's not worth
loving. Oh, no, no, I didn't mean that. I
didn't mean that. I didn't—' And the
tears. Then she wiped her eyes and blew

her nose. 'What a delightful evening I'm giving you!' she said. 'You have the patience of a saint. I wish I could be like you.'

'You wouldn't wish that if you knew.'

'I *do* know that you've been let down. You never get those phone-calls any more. But whatever happened I'll bet you took it on the chin or stiff-upper-lipped or something else very, very English. Huh! Laugh, Clown, laugh!'

'Let's have some supper,' I said.

'I couldn't eat a thing.'

I cooked eggs and bacon.

'That smells gorgeous,' she sighed and ate all I put before her. 'You *were* let down, weren't you, Auntie?' she said, as we drank more coffee after the meal.

'No love affair lasts for ever.'

'There you go! So calm, so philo-sophical. I wish I'd never been happy at all, then I'd never have had to feel like this. I haven't even any pride left. If I followed up my big ideas I'd kill myself, as Kate did, but I wouldn't have the nerve. I'm afraid of death. I'm afraid of life too. I dread tomorrow. And next week. And the week after.'

'You'll get by. You'll carry on with your work and put one foot in front of the other, until you're over it.'

'But there's a part of me that doesn't want to be over it, because I have nothing to put in its place—whatever "it" is. Without Tom, I don't care about anything. I've never felt like this before. There's always been hope before. Goodness, I'm starting off again. I must go. Oh, Auntie, thank you for being here. I do feel better than I did when I came. I can go home now and take some pills and sleep.'

'Don't take too many.'

'I wouldn't dare. Vicky the Yellow-belly, that's me. Cry, Clown, cry.' She pulled a weeping-clown face, to make me laugh, and off she went.

On the following afternoon a large bouquet of flowers was delivered to me, from a florist's shop. The attached card read: 'Just a little thank you for putting up with me. Vicky.' Then a P.S. in tiny writing: 'See you Monday.'

Monday came. I was half-glad of it, because work was my solace, yet dreading it too—Sam mourning the departed Jonquil; Vicky and Tom, lovers and enemies. The atmosphere would be electric.

When I did arrive, however, the atmosphere was stranger than even I had expected. There was a coldness, a lack of activity. Something was missing. It wasn't just the empty desks. Something—

The 'something' was that Hargon was away. The frosted glass kingdom was kingless. The silent power that emanated invisibly from it was not there. When God leaves his post what happens to his minions? Why wasn't he there? Holiday? He took holidays in theory, but rarely in practice. He loved the office. It was his home and his life.

His secretary was the person to ask. Very casually. 'Where's the Old Man today?'

'He's not coming in.'

'Oh. Why not? Is he ill?'

She gave me a wary look, then closed the door of her office which adjoined his. 'There's been a fire,' she said. 'His cottage was burned down last night.'

'The cottage where Kate—'

'Yes. He rang me at home early this morning.' She announced it proudly. *She* had been the one to receive vital information from high places. We journalists, who thought ourselves so clever and threw our weight about and received more wages than we deserved—we didn't know, did we? *She* knew.

'What happened then?' I asked her.

'I've just told you, haven't I? His cottage was burned down. He's away this morning because he's seeing to things.'

'Oh. I see.' Not that I did. She knew nothing really. Only the fact.

'I gather the Old Man's not here,' said Sam when I returned to my desk.

'No. I've just spoken to his secretary. Apparently the cottage was burned down and he's "seeing to things".'

Vicky came up. 'Where's the Old Man?'

The information was repeated and went round the whole office, of course. Wildfire, like a wild-cottage-burning.

'How could it catch fire if there was no one there?' said Vicky. 'Not that it matters.' Her eyes were swollen. She looked as if she'd been weeping all weekend. She

267

probably had. Tom was plodding about frozen-faced, like a moving statue. He carried an armful of luscious pin-ups as if they were a bundle of old newspapers. Which one day they would be of course. These poor little pin-up girls, I thought suddenly. Real people with real feelings, treated like that. Used. Tom tossed them down on his desk and began to plough through them, looking for 'innocent eyes', presumably. His own eyes were strangely innocent this morning. Bewildered. Young. Pain-filled.

'Thank you for the flowers,' I said softly to Vicky.

'It was a pleasure, Auntie.' Eyes remote. Pain-filled. Sam's eyes. Pain-filled. Too much pain. In the washroom I looked in the mirror at a reflection of my own eyes. Fleetingly I saw pain there too. I must be careful not to let people see my eyes. They're windows. Maybe I'll get some dark glasses. Pull down the blinds. Don't let anyone see...

A quiet morning, but for the tapping of typewriters. Sam frantically turning out more and more. 'Questions-and-Answers'. Vicky catching up on her film stuff. Tom still glaring at pin-ups. Kate sitting occasionally at her empty desk, there only when one wasn't looking, vanishing under direct gaze. Dave had missed the 'little fire' of her hair burning in our corner...

How had the cottage burned down?

When the lunch-hour came Tom walked over to Vicky, touched her on the shoulder and said something. She looked up at him and she smiled. Sunshine on wet ground. He'd asked her out for lunch! They left, hand-in-hand. No more pretences. They didn't care who saw. Vicky looked *happy*. 'So seize we the present and gather its flowers...'

After this week they would be flowers on a coffin of frustrated love. They did love each other, those two, although they didn't very much like each other. The tricks that Pan can play!

'Did those two have a row and make it up?' Sam asked me, watching them.

'Yes. Tom's leaving at the end of the week.'

'Oh, poor Vicky!' he said, in heart-felt tones, and asked for no details, which wasn't like Sam.

'How are things at home?' I enquired.

'I am sinking,' he said, 'gradually, back into the ooze. Which is where I belong.' And he went on with his 'Questions-and-Answers', slogging away. He had to get his column back into the paper! Otherwise where would his job be? At least, at the moment, he could pay the rent for the ooze he'd sunk back into. Ooze is expensive stuff. An out-of-work man can't afford ooze.

In the afternoon Hargon came back. He sent for me.

'Sit down, sit down.' He gestured towards a chair. 'Smoke if you like.' I did.

'My secretary told you about the cottage?'

'That it was burned? Yes.'

'Can you guess how it happened?'

'You did it?'

'Right! It was evil. There was something wrong there. Always has been, always would have been. I kept on *seeing* that poor girl. So I went down there yesterday afternoon, cleared out some of my private stuff and then, instead of putting the place up for sale, I sprinkled paraffin around and set light to it. It made a marvellous bonfire. Flames soaring to the sky. And I saw something. An outline of a hanged figure, on a gibbet. Clear as clear against the flames. Extraordinary!'

'But that was Sam's dream—' I told him of the content of Sam's dream and how Kate had been connected with it, which was why Sam had telephoned that time—that terrifying time—

'Mmm,' grunted the Old Man. 'There must be more to old Local Government, eh-by-gum Sam, than meets the eye.'

'Then you'd better put his column back in the paper next week.'

'That,' he said, 'is for me to decide, not you. Still, maybe he'll be better since that little tart left.'

'She wasn't!'

'I know she *wasn't,* but they're the worst tarts of the lot. Heaven spare me from the cock-teasers. Sam was "properly taken in".'

'I didn't know you knew so much about us all.'

He looked surprised. 'It's part of my job,' he said. 'I don't interfere in the private lives of the staff but I usually know what's going on. Journalists are very emotional people, you know. Most of them are frustrated novelists or playwrights or poets and they're always crying for some moon or other. I haven't been immune from that sort of thing myself. By the way,' and he lowered his gaze, 'I owe you an apology.'

'For what?'

'I think you know.'

'That's all right, Mr Hargon. We weren't ourselves that night.'

'Depends what you mean by "ourselves". I have several selves. Anyway we were saved by the bell. Sam, no less.' He threw back his head and laughed and so did I.

Our laughter must have echoed through the air of the outside office, for when I came out of the Old Man's room everyone looked at me.

'Did I hear sounds of merriment between you and His Nibs?' asked Sam.

'Was he telling you dirty jokes?'

'No,' and I didn't tell him what we had been laughing at, which was mean of me really, as he'd have been fascinated.

'What did he want you for then?' Sam insisted, his curiosity aroused.

'Nothing much. He told me about the cottage. It's been burned right down.'

'Good. It wouldn't have been fit to live in after what happened.' He glanced at Kate's desk. 'I suppose someone else will be coming to sit there soon,' he said, then he looked wistfully across at Jonquil's empty desk on the far side of the glass wall. Jonquil had always been on the far side of a glass wall where he was concerned and he'd hurt himself so much, banging against it, like a bird which cannot even see the glass. 'It's a weary life,' he said.

Then something happened which made us all sit up. The swing doors at the far end of the office opened and an enormously fat woman walked in. She moved slowly and smoothly, taking small steps, as if afraid of overbalancing. She went to the Old Man's room and walked in without even knocking.

273

'Who was that?' said Vicky in an awed tone.

'Mrs Hargon,' said Tom.

'His *wife?*' shrieked Vicky, then clamped her hand over her mouth and shook with giggles. Sam was similarly affected. He put his head down on the typewriter, the way he had done once before, and his shoulders heaved. Everyone began to laugh, as silently as possible, although squeaks were coming out of Vicky and Sam.

'What's so funny?' I said reproachfully, trying not to laugh myself.

Sam turned a twisted, crimson, half-wet face towards me. 'Picture them,' he said. 'The poor devil must be swamped. Talk about once round him and twice round the gasworks.'

'I think you're very vulgar and unkind,' and then I nearly collapsed too. 'Journalists are very emotional people,' the Old Man had said. How right he was. But, goodness, had his wife always been like that, or had she once been slender and sylphlike, and then the mountain of flesh had covered the spare outline and the metamorphosis had been complete?

It was *not* funny. Why am I laughing? I'm not really. I'm crying inside. So is Sam and Vicky and even Tom.

After we'd recovered Sam said, 'Well, if ever I've said anything critical about the Old Man having fancy women I take it all back. I don't blame him.'

'You men,' said Vicky. 'It's much worse for her. No one can help being fat. Maybe I'll be like that one day. I eat too much already.'

The door of the Old Man's room opened and he and his wife came out together. He looked insignificant beside her, yet there was something kindly and chivalrous about the way he put his hand under her elbow as he escorted her out. We didn't even want to laugh any more.

'He's not a bad bloke, is he?' said Sam.

The office was silent when the Old Man returned on his own. He was probably quite unaware of the sensation his wife had caused by her visit. After all, he saw her every day, so he would hardly 'see' her at all.

'I wonder what she came for,' said Vicky.

'Maybe she found a pair of Fanlight Fanny's pants in his bottom drawer,' suggested Sam, and Dave, who was near-by, gave a great belly-laugh and nearly dropped the cups of tea he had been bringing to Sam and me.

But maybe Sam was not so far off the mark, for a second later La Bellen wafted, much behatted, into Hargon's office.

'It's as good as a play,' said Sam.

'Oh, shut up!' said Vicky. 'Don't make me laugh again or I'll cry my eyes out!'

But the 'play' continued. It was like one of those avant-garde plays in which you haven't the faintest idea what it's about yet feel compelled to go on look-ing; for a few minutes later La Bellen and the Old Man came out together and left the office.

'His wife's going to sue for divorce,' said Sam, 'and Fanlight Fanny is the "woman named".'

'When he's free,' said Vicky, 'he can marry me and I will live in luxury and forget all about rotten old photographers who go and bury themselves in the pro-vinces,' at which Tom rose from his

276

desk and got her by the scruff of the neck. They wrestled, like lovers.

'Do you mind, children!' Hargon's secretary had risen up through the floor, apparently, like a pantomime character, for there she was.

'As soon as he leaves you all behave like kids when the teacher is out of the room,' she snapped. 'Message for you, Sam.'

Sam looked up with vulnerable hope— had Jonquil rung the office and sent him a message?

'He says your copy has been dull lately,' said the secretary, 'and will you get a really *good* set of "Questions-and-Answers" ready for the coming issue.'

'I'll do my best,' said Sam.

'Message for you too, Tom. He doesn't like the pin-up you've chosen. Her feet are too big.'

'I could fine them down.'

'Not without chopping off the little toe on each foot. We thought of that.'

'Our readers would not notice an eight-toed pin-up,' said Vicky. 'That's not the part they look at.'

'The foot-fetishists do,' I said. 'They

277

look at nothing else.'

'Auntie is a fund of filthy information,' said Sam.

'I don't know what's got into you lot today,' said Hargon's secretary and stalked away.

'Cow,' muttered Vicky. 'Poor old Hargon! A mountain for a wife and a battle-axe for a secretary. No wonder he's kinky.'

Then the nonsense died out of us as quickly as it had arisen and we worked sombrely until the end of the afternoon. As Sam left he said: 'Only Monday and I feel dead-beat already. Roll on Friday!'

'Friday is not going to come,' said Vicky. 'I forbid it. There are to be no more Fridays ever, starting with this one —and then you'll have to stay here for ever,' she told Tom.

But Friday did come for all that. Tom's last day.

CHAPTER 14

Vicky came 'dressed to kill'. She was going to make sure he didn't forget her. She looked marvellous. 'Whew!' said Sam. 'You look more like lunch at the Savoy than a day at the office.'

'He is taking me out to lunch. I am going to behave beautifully. No tears, no scenes, the perfect lady. Like Auntie. Ai shell iven speak with an Inglish eccent, lake the Queen and Peggy Eshcroft.'

'You're a card,' said Sam.

She showed me the present she had bought for Tom, a leather wallet with his initials on it. 'So that every time he gets out his money he'll have to think of me,' she said, reverting to her natural accent, 'and so will that cow of a wife and all the little baby cattle she bears, charging madly round ye olde English fields. I think I'm dying. Does it show?'

'No, darling, you look beautiful.'

'Auntie, if you get sentimental and

make me spoil my eye make-up I'll murder you.'

'Get on with your work then,' I said.

'I will do that thing.' Grim-lipped now, she got on with her work. It was made easier for her because Tom was not in the office. He was busy in the dark-room, leaving everything ship-shape for the new photographer who would start on Monday.

A rumour escalated to brighten the morning. The telephonists had gathered some titbits. It seemed that Mrs Hargon had come here the other day because she had found some feminine garment when she was unpacking the suitcase of odds-and-ends which Hargon had collected from the cottage before the fire. She knew it wasn't hers as it was too small. So she had trundled along to ask her husband whose it was. He had said that of course it must be Kate's, although if it had been it was odd that he'd handed it over to La Bellen and then taken her out for a drink.

'Honestly, the way people carry on,' said Sam, who, of course, had never 'carried on' in his life, to his deep regret.

The lunch-hour came. Tom emerged from the dark-room. 'Ready?' he said to Vicky.

'I'm ready. Tell me I look nice.'

He couldn't speak. They went out together.

'Poor devils,' said Sam.

Rain began to pour down, a cold summer storm of it, tapping on the windows, dancing on the pavements. The sunny afternoon in Hyde Park was a world away. I dashed across the road to the pub for a solitary drink. When Vicky came back to the office she would come alone. Tom had the afternoon off, as it was his last day. I was afraid that after the performance she'd put on for him she's crack up completely. You can act for just so long...you can bear up for as long as the drama keeps going, because it isn't quite real, but at curtain-fall—the dark. And *that* is real.

Afternoon work began and Sam and I waited for Vicky. She hadn't returned by three-thirty and we grew uneasy. 'She wouldn't do anything foolish, would she?' he said. 'It can happen so impulsively.' He knew just how impulsively.

At four o'clock, I said: 'Maybe she couldn't face the office and went home.'

'Ring her and see,' said Sam. 'Do you know her number?'

I found it in my address-book and dialled it. There was no reply. 'I don't see that we can do anything, Sam. She may have just gone for a walk.'

'In this rain?'

'Yes. In a weird way the rain would help.'

And that turned out to be true. To our vast relief Vicky turned up shortly before five, soaked through, her make-up all washed away, her pretty clothes ruined.

'I got wet,' she said.

'You'll catch pneumonia if you're not careful,' I exclaimed.

'I wouldn't mind.'

I hurried her into the washroom, helped her to take off her drenched clothes and she dried herself with some difficulty on the roller-towel. Mrs Bellen, proving unexpectedly sympathetic, provided a sweater and trousers which had been used for the dressmaking section of the Woman's Page and which fitted Vicky nicely. Clean and unpainted and wearing the simple outfit, Vicky looked like a little girl. She went to her desk, as if it were a home, and sat there, doing nothing.

Hargon came in and noticed her. 'Vicky—go home whenever you like.'

'Thank you, Mr Hargon,' but she didn't move.

He walked over to me, pretended to discuss some work, then whispered, 'See that she's all right, will you?'

I nodded.

'I saw her from my window, when she was coming back,' he continued softly. 'I hardly recognised her.' He shook his head a little and we both glanced down at the issue of the paper which was lying on my desk and from which Vicky's happy face smiled up at us—the face of a woman lying on the grass in the park, gazing into her lover's eyes. It was a different person from the beaten little figure crouched at its desk.

The rain stopped. Sam opened a window. A breeze blew in. Vicky shivered and turned. Sam said quickly, 'Oh, sorry, Vicky. Is there a draught on you? He began to close the window again.

'It doesn't matter,' she said. 'Nothing matters any more.'

By six the main office had emptied out. There was only Vicky and I left. 'I'm going home,' she said.

'Quite time too. Would you like me to come with you?'

'I mean I'm going *home*—back to Canada. I shall write to my folks tonight and leave at the end of the month. They love me, you know, strange as it may seem. I have never been grateful enough. I shall make it up to them now. Don't look at me so anxiously, Auntie. I'm not Kate. She didn't have any folks. I have.'

'Good. And shall you be all right alone tonight?'

'Yes. I shall write to them, as I said. Look what he gave me.' She drew her handbag towards her and extracted a little box containing a tiny ivory figure. It was a Netsuke ivory, exquisitely carved, of an old Japanese peasant with a face full of courage, stoicism and controlled pain. 'Isn't that just like Tom,' she said, 'to choose something that I can keep for ever and always love. I have no regrets.

Good-night, Auntie. See you Monday.' She went off in her borrowed clothes, her handbag in one hand and the little ivory figure clasped in the other. Her discarded finery still lay across a chair in the washroom, dry now but crumpled. I folded the garments carefully, as if they belonged to someone who had died. In a sense they did. She would never wear that outfit again. I found myself suddenly in tears for Vicky, who was past weeping.

Mrs Bellen came in. 'What's the matter?' she said. 'Oh, I suppose you're crying over some man. Never cry over a man, my dear. Not one of them is worth it.' And she took off her hat.

I stared. I had never seen her without a hat before.

She was examining herself in the mirror. 'This damned alopecia,' she said, rubbing a bald patch. 'As soon as one patch grows some hair on it another starts up. Do you have that sort of trouble?'

'I did once. It made me very miserable. Then the hair grew white on the bald patches and gave me a piebald look.'

'Men are so lucky being able to go bald

without it mattering,' she sighed. She was different tonight, ordinary and quite pleasant. She must have got very tired putting on that act of being a sort of 'glamour girl' all day. Underneath it she was like any other lonely middle-aged woman, earning her living, keeping up appearances, and finished with love, because love had finished with her.

As I left she called after me: 'Goodnight. Don't cry over him any more, whoever he is. They're all the same. They love you and leave you. The bastards!'

She had quite cheered me up, the very last person I would have expected to do so. I remembered those horrible bald patches I'd had myself, how I'd scuttled about for weeks with a scarf over my head, feeling less than the dust. Vanity, vanity. Poor Mrs Bellen. I would definitely *not* tell Sam. He'd laugh. For in certain respects men *are* all the same.

Then I thought of Rawden. He should be back from Sweden by now and it would be helpful to tell him some of the events that had occurred during his absence, otherwise he'd get a fearful shock when he arrived on Monday and found everything so changed—indeed devastated. Yes, I must tell him about Kate. Better for him to learn of it quietly on the telephone from me than to hear a variety of tales from the men's washroom as soon as he arrived. So when I reached home I looked up his number and dialled it. The ringing sound went on for such a long time that I began to think he wasn't back after all.

At last the receiver was lifted, however, and a voice repeated the number. It was a girl's voice. She had a Swedish accent. I heard Rawden's voice in the background: 'Oh, leave it. Come back to bed.' Gently I replaced the receiver.

So, I thought, the chase was not in vain. He's brought Ingrid back with him. I changed my mind over telling him about Kate. Let him enjoy the last weekend of his holiday without interruption. He'd have to take his chance on Monday as to how he received the dark news. At least his today was bright. At least one of our little 'family' had got his heart's desire. Oh, how slushy I'm getting. It's that column I write. I never escape from 'emotional problems' and it's wearing me down. Yet what else could I do? I hadn't the panache to be a reporter, nor the flair and style to work for the Woman's Page—not that I'd want to—heaven forbid! All that twaddle about clothes and cooking. I'd rather have my 'lonely hearts' than that. No, having become 'Auntie' on the staff, I was unfitted for anything else. Maybe I could leave journalism altogether and do social work; but you have to be qualified for that and anyway the pay is rotten. Also I wouldn't care for the responsibility or the actual presence of the many moaners. Do-gooding was out. I simply wasn't good.

I sat down and looked at the telephone. Silently it sneered. I thought of the hours I had spent over the years, waiting for it to ring, and how quite often he'd promised to ring and hadn't. And now whenever it rang I still hoped with that hopeless hope. Why then did I allow it to torment me so? Why keep a pet that is nothing but a misery-maker? I returned to an idea I'd had before: to get rid of it. Such a simple thing to do. Yet terribly difficult. But I *would* do it. Now!

Before I had time to weaken I wrote a letter to the Telephone Controller of the district, asked for my telephone to be disconnected straight away and added that they could call for 'the instrument' at their convenience. I reread the letter and found that by some Freudian slip I had written 'the instrument of torture', so the letter read as if I were asking to have a rack or thumbscrew removed from the loo. Oh, dear! I rewrote the letter, omitting 'of torture' and altering 'at your convenience' to 'when you have time'. By now I was feeling far from fraught than my simple action warranted and because of this I went out to post the letter straight away. If I didn't it would haunt me all night and I might even tear it up in the morning.

As I dropped it into the nearest pillar-box I whispered: 'That's the end of it, darling. After this weekend you'll never be able to ring me at home again, even if you wanted to.'

You're a fool. He never would anyway. He doesn't want to.

You can shut up, whoever you are. Leave me alone.

You'll be left alone all right. Fancy having the phone cut off because someone does *not* ring! It's mad. If you were being pestered it would be understandable.

You don't understand.

You're right I don't!

Which of you is me?

We both are.

'I must stop talking to myself,' I said aloud and a passer-by gave me a funny look and I tried to appear as if I had not spoken, which was pretty silly as people look the same when they haven't spoken as when they have. Laugh, Clown, laugh...

Vicky would be writing to her parents now. Sam would be having supper and making conversation with his wife. Tom would be having supper and making conversation with *his* wife. Rawden would still be in bed. And Kate? The inquest was over. A cremation had been arranged. Fire into the fire. Brave Kate. I began to 'see' her again as I walked in the dark, but the vision was already becoming less frequent and as soon as someone new came to sit in her desk her evasive little ghost would be banished. The dead are so very dead. We do not go on remembering.

What shall I do with the rest of my life?

Your egotism makes me sick. What's so special about *your* life?

No one can live for me.

So what? Self-pity, self-pity.

If I don't pity myself no one else is going to bother!

And why bloody should they?

'Oh, shut up!' I said aloud.

'She's drunk,' said a passer-by to her companion.

I wasn't in the least drunk but it was a good idea. I looked for a pub. As I'd been wandering aimlessly I wasn't sure where I was. It was rather pleasant being 'lost'. A letting-go feeling. A pub, a pub, my kingdom for a pub...as a child, and ice-cream addict, I and a little friend had sometimes wandered along the street together chanting: 'Walls, Walls, please come here, Eldorado, do appear,' and maybe we were miniature witches, for, sure enough, in due course, a Walls or Eldorado ice-cream-van *would* appear...

And now a pub did. I went in and ordered a double vodka.

I paid for it, smiled nicely and the barman said: 'Thank you, madam.'

Then Madam sat down with her drink and was aware of glances. It's always the same if a female goes alone into a pub. We get the swift once-over. A relic of bygone times. It wouldn't happen in a coffee-bar. It's strange and rather sad. It makes you feel self-conscious when you wanted to relax. It's not that anyone bothers you. It's just that initial *look* that takes the easiness out of things. So I drank my drink fairly quickly and went out again to find my way home. I couldn't be all that far away. I'd only been walking. But when you walk without looking or thinking about where you are you can get lost near home. And what is home anyway? If it isn't inside yourself it's nowhere. The complete person is at home wherever he is.

All very well to philosophise, but in doing so I became more lost than ever and grew practical. I must find my flat again! I needed to pee, for a start. Then I saw a familiar bus number. Oh, yes—of course—we were on our way—

We reached the flat in due course, my other self and me. We used the lavatory and made coffee. We looked at the telephone and said to it: 'You haven't much longer to live.'

And then I felt sorry for it. My sufferings had not been its fault, poor little *Nevermore* raven. 'All the same,' I told it, 'you're going to be disconnected and that means dying. Do you mind?'

It sat there so meekly. It did mind! It's a person! Perhaps, for a machine, 'being a person' is an infectious illness, as love, suicide, scabies and measles are infectious illnesses for people. Who knows? Had my poor little raven caught humanity from me?

You know your thoughts are those of a madwoman.

I've been mad for a long time.

What with?

Love.

Then why are you cutting off the lifeline to love?

Because it was a deathline.

You'd better go to bed.

At last we agree.

My various selves gathered themselves together and went to bed, as if they were one. They even slept. In the morning they went shopping and behaved very well. They bought coffee, bread, butter, eggs and cheese. They were intent on survival, although they had no idea what they were surviving *for*. Except perhaps for the ever-changing sky and the ever-shimmering river and the leaves on the trees and the leaf-shadows on the pavement and the utter glorious beauty of God's world—which we never appreciate enough, because we shut ourselves up in self-prisons and peer through gratings of the mind...

I lived through the weekend in a dream and the doomed telephone lived with me, reproaching me. But I had done the deed. My letter was posted. I wouldn't give in.

'You're only symbolic!' I told it.

It looked at me, with pain.

Monday morning I left it. Left it with a shrug of the shoulders. I was 'Auntie' this morning. I was going to work. The doomed pet would be left to die alone. Or maybe they wouldn't cut its lifeline today, but tomorrow. When would the

Telephone God receive my letter and how soon would he act afterwards? It might still be alive when I came back. Or it might not.

I sat in the Underground train, still haunted by it.

When I reached the office I felt tired out. I was early. I sat down at my desk in the corner. Everything was still unreal. I saw Kate sitting in front of me, her red hair aflame, although the morning was grey. 'Kate,' I whispered.

She turned, smiled and vanished.

'Hello, Auntie. You're early.'

The familiar Strine voice breaking through the clouds of insanity and bringing me right down to earth.

'Rawden! Hello! Good to see you.'

'Good to see you too. Glad the old firm's still ticking over.' He sat down at his desk. Other members of staff began to arrive.

Rawden turned to me. 'Where's Kate then?' he said. 'Or did she and Andrew get spliced while I was away?'

Spliced. Sliced.

'Hasn't anyone told you?'

'No. What's been going on?'

'They're both dead.'

'What! What happened? Car crash?'

I couldn't bear to describe the events to him, to see, underlying his horror, that gleam of journalistic avidity, that unheard whisper: What a story!

'Here's Sam. He'll tell you.'

'About Jonquil?' said Sam. 'Yes, she's left, Rawden.'

'I want to know about Kate and Andrew,' said the other.

Sam lowered his voice and began to tell the long, sad tale. Now that the initial shock had worn off he quite enjoyed recounting it. Then Rawden asked: 'What's happened to Tom?' for a stranger was at Tom's desk.

'He's left too,' said Sam. 'He left on Friday and Jonquil the Friday before that.'

'So welcome back to Heartbreak Corner,' said Vicky, who had just come in, dressed in black. 'Look at me,' she declaimed. 'I am in mourning for my life, like that character in Chekhov.'

'Poor old Vick,' said Rawden. 'What a bloody shame!'

'How about you then?' said Sam.

296

'How was Sweden? Tell us all.'

Rawden said calmly: 'There was a wedding.'

CHAPTER 15

'You and Ingrid are married?' I said. 'Oh, congratulations!'

'Ingrid is married, Auntie. I was not the bridegroom. All I did at the wedding was get drunk at the reception. But it turned out quite well, in a way. I got acquainted with one of the bridesmaids and brought her back to England with me to share the flat. Man was not meant to live alone.'

'Do you love her?' Vicky asked.

'Love Greta? No. I'm through with all that. I'm never going to make a fool of myself over a woman again.'

'To make love without loving *is* making a fool of yourself. It is also wrong,' said Vicky.

'Look who's moralising!' Rawden protested. 'A man must have a sex life or he gets frustrated. Read any psychiatric text-book.'

'I don't care,' said Vicky. 'It's still wrong. I know it is because I used to do it, but once you've made love with love you know it's right and that the other was wrong. Sam agrees with me, don't you, Sam?'

'Sam is a married man. He doesn't have to be frustrated,' said Rawden.

'Most married men,' said Sam, 'are a damned sight more frustrated than single ones if you really want the truth.'

'Then that's their own fault,' said Rawden. 'They should train their wives better.'

'Try telling that to my wife,' said Sam.

'Any time,' nodded Rawden.

Sam laughed. 'Eh, I don't know! You youngsters!'

'I'm not young,' said Rawden. 'I'm old, cynical and disillusioned.' And behind all his brash remarks there was a sadness and that look of pain had not left his eyes.

How different people were over being 'crossed in love'! Vicky dramatised it, but it had softened her: Rawden was undramatic but hardened, albeit surfacely; Sam was philosophical, or trying to be; and I mostly kept quiet and went mad inside my own head. I kept thinking of the doomed telephone. Had they cut its lifeline yet? Would it emit a final little 'ping' of agony? Symbolic, symbolic. A slight case of crackpot transference. I was transferring my own feelings into a machine. I caressed the sides of my typewriter. Dear little friend, so patient and hardworking, always here waiting for me. I had a typewriter at home too. Another friend. A good companion.

Rawden said: 'Auntie seems to be the only one of us who isn't tearing her hair.'

'She has her troubles too but she doesn't go on about it the way we lot do,' said Sam. 'Oh, we haven't told you about Hargon's wife and Fanlight Fanny, Rawden—' And they were gossiping again.

Then Hargon sent for me. 'Sit down. Smoke if you want to. I've got an idea I want to discuss with you.'

He was very spruce and businesslike this morning and his eyes had a truly editorial gleam as he propounded his 'idea'.

'This story—this "tragic romance", you might call it—of Kate and Andrew. I want it written up truthfully as to facts, but imaginatively, as if it were fiction. I can't think of any of the reporters who would handle it with the sort of emotion I want, so will you do it? No names, of course. Give the characters invented names. And make the lovers' first meeting at some other place of work—not a newspaper office. You could make them P.R.O's. It's a marvellous love story, you know. Quite Shakespearean. We don't have enough about *love* in the paper. There's plenty of sexual titilation in the pin-ups and the cartoons and there's practical advice about marriage and kids and so on—and there's the occasional "romantic" short story, which somehow never rings true and strikes an old-fashioned note. None of it goes deep. How do you feel about it? Will you write it for me?'

I was so surprised that I didn't answer immediately.

'Am I asking too much?' he said. 'I

know how distressed you've been and that Kate was your friend—but that very fact makes you the right person to handle the story. Well?'

'Yes. Yes, I'll do it. I think I would even like to.' And I was suddenly very excited, for it would be something good to create out of events which, in themselves, contained so much sorrow, and horror. The story was framing itself in my thoughts all day, although surfacely I did my usual chores in connection with the column and spoke to people when they spoke to me. I was there yet not there. Sam, Vicky and Rawden became shadowy compared with Kate and Andrew. But I didn't attempt to start the story at the office. I wanted to be alone when I wrote it.

As soon as I reached my flat that evening, I made coffee and sat down at my own typewriter. For a second I was almost afraid to begin in case I found the task beyond me. I smoked two cigarettes before I could type the first line. Then, having begun, I found that the ice was broken and I simply went on. I went on for hours. The story 'wrote itself', in that

I identified with the lovers, became them, each in turn, then together, and Kate received more attention than Andrew because I knew her better. How much objective truth there was in the result and how much of it was only my fragmented self parcelled up in words I couldn't know. All I did know was that it *felt* right when I was doing it and that when I read it through afterwards I had that uncanny feeling of: Who wrote this?

What time was it? Midnight. Goodness, and I hadn't even had any supper. Another thing: I had completely forgotten about the telephone. Had it been disconnected yet? I lifted the receiver to test it. It was dead. It had died alone, in the daytime, when I was out. I had sat with its corpse all evening and hadn't even noticed, because I was working. Real, exciting work. Quite different from the pap I handed out in my column. Had I actually found something to 'replace love'? I remembered the Old Man saying that most journalists were 'frustrated novelists, playwrights and poets'. But why *be* frustrated? A lover may be frustrated when his beloved doesn't love back, but to throw yourself into a novel which you are writing you need no other person. You can have your 'love affair' all by yourself. Why don't I do some 'real writing' in my spare time? Why didn't I think of it before? Too busy thinking of *him,* I suppose.

Suddenly ravenous, I ate a lot of bread, butter and cheese and a tomato, then drank more coffee, smoked more cigarettes and checked my story again. By two in the morning it was ready, only messy with alterations. I would have to do a fair copy tomorrow. Today, rather. I went to bed and set my alarm for five o'clock. When it rang I got up eagerly, made coffee, lit a cigarette and reread the story. It was—good? Was it? Doubts suddenly. Never mind, you can't judge your own work. It's your best, even if it isn't good. Don't shilly-shally. Type it out.

By the time it was finished I had to leave for the office. As soon as I arrived I took the story to Hargon's room and laid it on his desk.

'What are you up to, leaving billy-duxes for the Old Man?' asked Sam.

'It's only a story he asked for.'

'You look like death,' he said.

'I feel fine.' But I didn't any more. I felt dreadful. Exhausted. Shaking. Slightly sick. All that coffee and tobacco and typing and eating cheese in the small hours—poor old Auntie's inside was in a turmoil. Yet I couldn't relax. I was waiting for Hargon to arrive. When I saw him enter his room I could have passed out. I felt as if I'd left something utterly precious on his desk—and if he spurned or scorned it—if he did—

I simply don't know how I managed to dictate my letters during the next hour or so. Some robot must have taken over.

At last a figure of doom approached me in the form of Hargon's secretary.

'He wants you,' she said.

'Aren't you lucky!' joked Rawden.

'Out goes Fanny and in goes Auntie,' said Sam. 'Don't do anything I wouldn't do.'

'You queer then, Sam?' said Rawden.

'Do you men have to talk like smutty little schoolboys?' demanded Vicky.

'We are offending the virginal Victoria, Sam,' said Rawden.

Their chattering was no more than noisy air to me. I walked like a zombie to the Old Man's room and tapped on the door.

'Come!'

I opened the door and stood in the doorway.

He was working hard at his desk. 'Ah!' He looked up. 'Yes! Thought you'd like to know straight away.' He held up my story. 'Absolutely first-rate,' he said.

'Oh, thank you, Mr Hargon!'

'Thank *you.*' He nodded my dismissal. I closed the door gently behind me, as if it were fragile, fragile as a happy moment. For I was so happy at that moment—happy with my eyes full of tears.

Through the blur of tears I looked across to Kate's empty desk. She was there. She smiled, beautifully, and I hurried towards her, blinking my tears away—but of course when I reached the corner, clear-eyed, she was not there.

In the afternoon Vicky asked me: 'Is it true that you've written a story about Kate and Andrew, for the paper?'

'Yes.'

She looked shocked. 'I couldn't believe it when Hargon's secretary told me. Auntie, how could you! Using a real person like Kate for a story in this—this rubbishy rag of a paper.'

'Steady on,' said Sam. 'We all work on this "rubbishy rag".'

'And we should be ashamed of ourselves,' said Vicky.

'You're getting just too puritanical to live with,' said Rawden.

'Well, you don't have to live with me, thank God! How's the gorgeous Greta?'

'Good in bed,' said Rawden.

'You're just a nasty old Strine goat!' flared Vicky.

'Your words do not become your black garb,' said Rawden. 'When are you going to start dressing like a human being again? I miss your lovely legs and plunging necklines.'

'You!' Vicky punched him in the chest.

And it all went on round me like a play. So Vicky was critical of what I'd done? I didn't care. But although Vicky was the outspoken one she wasn't the

306

only one who was critical. Sam was a bit shocked too, as if I'd shown a certain lack of decency. Had I? I still didn't care!

Out of the blue Sam said later: 'She'd have been away on holiday now anyway.' He meant that Jonquil had been taking the first two weeks in July for her holiday. He still remembered that. He was by no means 'over it'. He was staring so sadly at the empty desk on the far side of the glass.

Vicky, I noticed, was making no attempt to befriend the new photographer who sat in Tom's desk, although he was a handsome chap. It wasn't that she had anything against him personally but his very presence wounded her, so she left the 'hail-fellow-well-met' stuff for the members of staff sitting on the other side of him. He wouldn't mind. To him Vicky was merely a girl in black who spoke with a Canadian accent and kept squabbling with the Australian reporter. Our little corner had become even more self-contained—although, let's face it, 'Auntie' was not quite so popular as she had been. Not so trustworthy maybe?

After all, they must have thought, suppose she starts writing about *us!*

And that, in my secret heart, was just what I was thinking of doing. If I wrote a novel I could use *them* as characters. Already I had become a sort of spy in the camp and they sensed it. I would start my novel of office life at the weekend, two free, uninterrupted days. Solitude and dead telephone. Marvellous! It was almost like being in love! And then—Oh, bliss!—my own holiday fortnight would be the third and fourth weeks in July and I hadn't known what to do with it—had been rather dreading it—now I longed for it. I would shut myself in my flat, make the world go away and write.

The weekend came. On Saturday morning I sat down to work. As when I'd started the story about Kate and Andrew I was afraid to put down the first line, but once it was written some influence seemed to take me over and carry me on. There was only one interruption—a man came for the telephone. When I watched him finally detach the raven's corpse from the wall I did feel a pang, but he was very quick and businesslike and the operation was soon over. He scuttled out again as if he were afraid of me, probably because when he usually detached phones it would be due to the customer's not having paid his bill. Rotten job for the bloke, when you come to think of it. Not that I cared. I returned to my typewriter and went on working.

The weekend, usually so dragging and dreary, passed in a flash. On Monday I'd have given anything not to go to the office, to stay here instead and get on with my book. But that was not to be. Anyway, only one week to get through now before my holiday. How exciting it was! I suppose this is a kind of madness, the way I'm carrying on—but I don't care!

I did care a little, however, that it was Vicky's last week as far as I was concerned. By the time my holiday was over she would have gone back to Canada. I would miss her. I cared too when I saw a young man sitting in Kate's desk. He was the photographer who would be taking her place. He was pleasant enough and Sam looked after him, showing him where the washroom was and feeding him with titbits of gossip about the Old Man and Fanlight Fanny. All so silly! The newcomer 'broke' our corner and Vicky's departure would break it even more. Already it belonged to the past. But I was giving it permanent life in my book. Heartbreak Corner would live on in words. Nothing that had happened would be wasted.

On the Friday Sam said: 'If she hadn't left she'd be back next week, but I wouldn't have been here to see her, because I'm off next week myself.'

'You and me both,' I said.

'Let's take Vicky out to lunch,' he suggested. 'We shan't see her again.'

'Super idea!'

Sam looked at me in a puzzled way, then said: 'Have you got together with *him* again? No, don't look so startled. I don't know who he is and I'm not asking, but I've noticed that your telephone calls stopped and I thought it was over, because you looked so down-in-the-mouth sometimes, but now—*have* you got together with him, or with someone else?'

'No.'

'Oh. My mistake.' But he wasn't convinced and I wasn't going to tell him that my 'secret lover' was not a man but a book. Devious old Auntie. I should be ashamed.

We took Vicky out to lunch. She talked about Tom and Sam talked about Jonquil. They both became quite tearful. As we finished Sam said, 'When Auntie and I come back from our holiday everything will be different. I expect Rawden will leave quite soon too. He's not the sort to stay in one place for long. We've been like a little family, haven't we?' and Vicky, who had drunk a lot of wine, said: 'You've been like a father to me, Sam.'

'Steady on, I'm not all that old!' he protested. 'Eh, if ever a man suffered!'

When we returned from lunch the advance copies of the coming issue of the paper were ready. Dave distributed them. My 'Love Story', as the editor had headlined it, had been given a centre spread and a very good illustration by one of the artists.

'That,' said Dave, pointing to it, 'is the best thing that's ever been written in this paper.'

Vicky said: 'Yes, it is good, Auntie. I'm sorry if I was nasty about it before. It *is* good. It's sincere. It almost makes me cry.'

Sam said: 'I don't honestly think you should have done it, but seeing that you did, well, it could hardly be better done.'

'You'll find yourself writing a novel one day, Auntie,' Rawden commented, with a laugh, and I, double-faced, laughed at the absurdity of such an idea.

While at home my novel was sitting there waiting for me. Come on, hurry up, it was silently calling. Let's get on with it!

I went home at six o'clock prompt and got on with it. My plan was to do as much of the first draft as possible during my leave, while everything was so fresh in my mind. I wouldn't reread and check meticulously as I went, but get the first version down, then the checking could be done steadily in the evenings, after I was back at the office. I had sixteen free days and I would have a routine, making myself break off and rest at regular times, so that I wouldn't become exhausted and collapse before the finish. I was good at organising my office work. I must be equally efficient over this new venture. For it must be more than mere psycho-therapy, I warned myself, even though that's probably what it really is. It's a way of streaming my madness into creative channels instead of letting these self-conversations and near-hallucinations buzz around my head, useless and undisciplined. I shan't just write this book: I shall live it.

Plans don't often work, but on the whole this plan did. I worked steadily, day after day, and each morning on waking I was eager to return to the type-writer.

Only one thing happened to upset me. More than upset me. Terrify me momentarily out of my wits. And when I recall it I still shudder with remembered fear.

It happened towards the end of the second week of my holiday. I was ex-tremely tired but determined not to give in to that. I collapsed into bed at about one in the morning and woke again at three. What had wakened me? A noise... *that* noise...but it couldn't be...it was lit-erally impossible...the sound of the tele-phone ringing in the living-room.

CHAPTER 16

Petrified, I lay listening. The sound couldn't really be coming from my flat. There was no telephone here. Was it a new telephone in another flat in the house? No, that would be more distant. This was *in the next room*.

Either you've gone completely mad, or someone is playing a trick, or the place is haunted by poltergeists...You are going to get up and go in there and look...

I got up, my heart beating so hard and fast that I was breathless. I tiptoed to the bedroom door and opened it slowly. The ringing became louder. I turned on the light.

The ringing stopped.

I went over to the corner where the telephone had been. No telephone. The wiring was still set in the wall, but that could make no sound without being connected to a phone with a bell.

So it was a dream? It must have been a

dream. I thought I was awake but I wasn't really—that was it—

But I was awake. I had had a dream-awake.

I returned to bed and even slept again, because of this extreme tiredness. In the morning I convinced myself that I'd had a nightmare and had not risen from my bed at all. That would have been easier to believe if I hadn't left the living-room light on—but that could have been left on previously anyway.

Determinedly I put the incident out of my mind and got on with my work. As the day passed I forgot about the ringing of the telephone that wasn't there. Only when I went to bed that night did I remember it, with dread, and pray that it would not happen again. It did not. Nor did it happen the next night, nor the next, nor the next. Only a silly dream. What else?

On the Sunday evening before I was due back at the office I had almost finished my book. Almost. I had suddenly stuck. I had the time, in the hours left, to finish it in the rough. But it refused to finish. Maybe, I thought, something will happen, in real life, to give it an ending. But I still tried in vain to 'think up' an ending, instead of leaving it to 'real life'. The book had been so real up till now, however, that it refused to have anything invented for it out of my journalist's imagination. It was waiting for life to catch up with it. I had gone too fast...I had run past it...I had run out of 'real life'. I had simply sat in this nun's cell...

What was happening outside?

Anything to 'give me an ending'?

Well if there is anything it'll have to come of its own accord. The skeleton of the book is mostly there. I can take my time now. In evenings to come, after the office, I can check and recheck, rewrite where necessary, retype messy pages. And maybe an end will *come*. I went to bed, tired to death, but not unhappy, because the main work was done.

On Monday morning the thought of going back to the office with its comparatively simple chores was like a holiday. I needed a rest after this 'holiday'.

When I was about to leave the post

came. A letter dropped through the slit in the door as I was stepping that way. In fact I stepped *on* it, by a weird little co-incidence, a synchronicity of the letter's falling and my forward-stepping.

I picked it up, rather impatiently. It couldn't be important. Nothing was important except that I'd almost finished my skeleton-book and needed only an ending...

The address was written in unfamiliar handwriting. A woman's writing, I guessed. And I went cold, without knowing why, but sensing something...I tore the letter open.

I looked first at the signature: 'Yours sincerely,' and the name of *his* wife. Why was she writing to me? I'd behaved perfectly, hadn't I? I'd withdrawn from the situation, made no attempt to get in touch, obeyed all those diabolical rules that married men impose on their 'bits on the side'...What had she to complain about?

She wasn't complaining. She was merely informing me.

He was dead. A heart attack. So sudden. At three a.m.—yes, on *that* small-hours morning—when I had wakened and heard the non-existent telephone ringing and ringing and ringing—telling me—and I had been too self-obsessed to understand the message...

I looked at the manuscript on my desk and hated it. What's a pile of writing compared with love? Deep down I had never really stopped hoping, you see. There was always my office telephone. One day he might have rung and I'd have been able to tell him that I wasn't all that wet—that I'd written a novel!

I put the letter in my bag and went to the office. Sam said: 'You don't look as if your holiday's done you much good.'

'He's dead, Sam.'

'Who? Oh, *the* one? The one who stopped ringing?' I nodded, even though he'd rung, when it was impossible. 'Eh, lass, I'm sorry! Eh—I *am* sorry!'

Later I said to him: 'I'd probably never have seen him again anyway, but there was always the little hope, you know?'

'I know. I look for Jonquil wherever I go. One day I might see her, or my office phone might ring—'

'Yes. That's how it was. I got rid of my home telephone so that it wouldn't torment me, but there was still this one. I was fooling myself.'

'You'll get over it, you know.'

'I know.'

And that morning I dictated a letter to a recently bereaved widow, offering sympathy and adding a few platitudes about the healing power of time, which does exist, of course, but which is hard to believe in when—when—Oh, when does the healing begin?

You were only his mistress, you were not his wife. You only loved him, he didn't really love you. He had left you anyway, so your life will be no different. Thus I instructed myself. The little raven on my desk gave an unexpected squawk. *Nevermore.*

Work is the answer. As soon as I get home tonight I'll start the second draft of my book. I don't really hate it. It gave me happiness and it is something achieved, even if it's never published.

And that night, calm and determined, I sat down to work. I began to reread my book, checking and altering as I went. It began: 'We were all in love that year at the office...' And I even had an ending now. I'd only had to wait for the real event to happen. It had 'written itself for me'.